SLOW DOWN, PRINCESS!

"You have a female friend?" Cosmo injected with a quick smile and a demure glance at Saira. "A wife?"

Saira shot back an ice cold look of her own, but then jerked her head around to anxiously wait for Kaiden's answer.

"No. My father's... student. She cannot be... as wife... while she is a student."

"Oh, but... maybe when she's finished?" Cosmo nodded in encouragement, offering the natural possibility.

Kaiden looked slightly confused at Cosmo's tone for a moment, and looked back and forth between Saira and her attendant. Kaiden swallowed the bread in his mouth and for the second time in moments he looked as though he was worried he had said something wrong. "I... am surprised. The females are required to... be as wife?"

"No!" Saira expressed, irritated as she waved Cosmo quiet. "We decide who we are with, when and for how long. We don't let the males tell us what to do." She turned to look simply at Cosmo. "Or not to do."

Kaiden brightened. "Ah, well, it is... uh... com–pat–i–ble... with us. I am sorry, Mister Cosmo. I do not wish to make assumptions and Princess Saira has made me, perhaps, excited and eager to... talk. Learn more about your people."

"Oh, I'm excited and eager to learn more, too," Saira countered, softly, placing her elbows on the table and her chin on her closed hands as she gazed at the handsome ambassador.

Oh crap! Cosmo thought. *Crap! Crap! Crap!*

FLAMES of DESTINY

a story of Zefphyr

Kurt Kennett

Illustrations by Amber Scharf

www.zefphyr.com

ISBN 978-0-9968712-1-1

Manufactured in the United States of America.

First International LuLu.com edition: October 2015

For Weirdlet, Leam, Ceres and Depleti

preface

The people of Earth frowned on the scientists, branding their interests as incompatible with a just society. But the researchers wanted to continue their work, for it was all they had.

They went out into the blackness of space, sorting and poring over millions of worlds to find Zefphyr. They saw the cloudy, wind-swept planet as a haven and hideout - a sanctuary from prying eyes.

Zefphyr was different – strange and powerful. Wrapped in cloaks of harmonic energy that the scientists plundered with their machines and raped for their tests and their experiments. For their version of nature.

And they brought their flora, their fauna, workers and helpers, partners and children. But they found the planet inhabited by a precursor race. Felids – learning and growing, evolving on their own path with their own spirits and destiny.

The scientists took the rustic cats. Ripped them from their homes, molded them and genetically combined them with the other life forms the Humans had brought and created.

From all their animals and from themselves, the Masters took whatever they needed to follow their destiny. They made the seeds.

They were, to a one, driven. Cold.

But their servants and builders were not. The helpers saw the sentience in the seeds of life. Saw themselves in the genetic creations. Some broke away – ran away with the seeds they could save or steal. They could not let their brothers languish in servitude and slavery as toys.

And so began the struggle for control – a battle for life and death. For what was... humane. Heroes and villains rose and fell, until the eve of the greatest conflict. The greatest destruction.

The Meltdown.

All that the scientists had brought and built was destroyed – at once and finally, with the greatest of sacrifices. Only scattered remnants of technology and tools remained. All that were left struggled – some stumbled together, some apart. Across the planet the varieties spread and grew, changed and evolved.

For a thousand years.

one

Cosmo came down the stone steps of the palace tower and ambled his way through the back of the castle toward the kitchen. The Felid preferred silence and privacy first thing in the morning, and he had found that the small nook at the back of the kitchen larders with its solitary table and chair was one of the only truly quiet places available. As he wound his way past wooden tables and stacked dishes, he clutched his black attendant's robe to himself to prevent it from being caught on the handles of pots that stuck out as they simmered on the stoves.

He was expecting only a bowl of porridge to be waiting for him – Miss Kek the cook knew his schedule and prepared his morning meal so that it cooled to the exact temperature he preferred by the time he arrived. But when he came through the tiny doorway to his sanctuary he stopped and blinked at the three people crowded around his tiny table: Miss Kek was in the chair staring at Cosmo's breakfast in front of her; Mister Arfan the baker leaned against the table, thin arms crossed over his chest; and Mister Garro the groundskeeper stood next to the wall, picking dirt out from under his nails. As Cosmo appeared in the doorway they raised their eyes to him, but none of them spoke.

Cosmo's triangular face had high cheek bones and tawny yellow eyes barely visible beyond small, round wire rimmed glasses. He couldn't stop his brows from furrowing at the violation of his private space. The thin male Felid glared pointedly at each of them in turn, then used the index finger of his left hand to gently push his glasses up the bridge of his nose. "Am I interrupting something?"

"Mister Cosmo!" All three started at the same time, and all three stopped in deference to each other. Miss Kek raised herself from the chair and slid against the wall, beckoning with an arm to the small space she had vacated.

Cosmo slowly crossed his own arms over his chest but did not move to sit down. With a quick sigh he pointed at Miss Kek – she had, after all, made his breakfast and should go first. The short round Felid quickly nodded.

"Mister Cosmo, the big oven's broke! It ain't getting itself hot, just barely warm. The meat I gotta cook today ain't gonna sear and cook proper lest it's fixed."

Cosmo nodded calmly and shifted his gaze to Arfan, raising the same single finger to point to him in turn. Normally relaxed, then Human baker looked particularly out of sorts as he relayed his own problem.

"I got a bad batch of yeast. The sugar breads didn't rise last night. I could start again but they won't be ready in time for tonight."

Another pause and another slow nod. Garro didn't wait to be pointed at.

"Courtyard's a mess. Winds blew through last night and two flower pots on the parapet knocked over and done busted. Dirt's run everywhere and I can't lay out the–"

"Stop," Cosmo said flatly as he blinked and forced a smile. He took a step towards the table and rotated himself smoothly into the seat. He used the spoon to stir the rapidly cooling cereal mixture, then tentatively took a small portion to sample a bite. He smiled at the taste and temperature. "Where is your master?"

Silence.

"Where is House Master Darris?" He repeated, a bare wisp of fatigue in his voice. He took another bite of the cereal and savored it in his mouth.

"Master ain't been down yet," Miss Kek said. "I woke him at the first day mark, and he said he'd be down. But he ain't been down yet."

"Old fart's eighty cycles old," Garro mumbled quietly.

Miss Kek covered her mouth in surprise at the remark, and Cosmo stopped eating and peered sideways at the groundskeeper. Arfan swallowed and looked at the floor. Garro crossed his burly Kesten arms but did not qualify his comment.

Cosmo took a breath and blew it out his nose. "Mister Garro – you will move the dinner seating to the main hall chamber. Go see Captain Valaria and tell her I am asking for at least two of her guards to help you move the furniture and set up the hall. Do you understand?"

"Yes, Mister Cosmo." Garro shuffled sideways, bowed his head and began to exit the room.

"Wait – Mister Garro – you said two flower pots on the parapet are 'done busted'. Did you call the mason?"

"Yes, I called Miss Kella. She's done got here and is removin' the pieces now. Gonna make some new ones and bring 'em back in five days."

"Excellent. She helped build the master oven in the kitchen. Miss Kek – please accompany Mister Garro to find Miss Kella and ask her to come down and start immediate repairs to the oven. Whatever will get us through to tomorrow."

"Yes, Mister Cosmo," Miss Kek nodded, and quickly headed out the tiny doorway with the groundskeeper.

Cosmo took a large spoonful of his breakfast and closed his eyes as he chewed it. "Mister Arfan, you say you cannot make the sweet breads in time, even using new yeast?"

"No, Mister Cosmo." The baker sighed loudly. "Won't rise proper in time."

"Can you make something else?"

"Mister Cosmo, for her birthday princess prefers them sweet breads for everyone. She's been having 'em every cycle what... on nine cycles now. And can't stop talkin' about them every cycle afterwards. Dusted up right and pretty with that white cream icing and–"

"Yes, I know them. I ate four of them last cycle," he smiled. "Well, she's not going to get them this cycle, and she'll understand. It's not your fault, so don't feel bad. What else can you make in time?"

"Oh, I can make any number of pretty things that–"

"Excellent. Off you go. You choose. Both the princess and I trust you to make something special for her for tonight. You're good at what you do and you know what she likes. Be creative."

"Right. Thank you Mister Cosmo." Arfan pushed off from the table, turned and dipped his head slightly before leaving the room.

Cosmo closed his eyes took a deep breath, enjoying the sudden return of silence and privacy. But barely a moment had passed before a shadow signaled another visitor. Eyes still closed, he frowned and sighed loudly in exasperation. "What is it now?"

"I am sorry to intrude."

Cosmo jerked suddenly up to standing, eyes going wide as he dropped his spoon. It clattered on the table then fell onto the floor, making him wince at the sound. "Sire! Your Majesty!" he blurted.

King Tharn smiled as he stood in the doorway, his tall frame easily filling the portal. Dressed in his normal double–breasted white robes, the black and tan Felid clasped his hands behind his back, strong shoulders pulled wide. His outfit was padded with layers of soft fabric on top of his thin fur and skin. Thick black–hide boots covered his long legs from the knee down, and the white cape that he wore came down to just above the floor. Everyone knew that the northern felids were descendants of genetic recombination between the Human 'Masters' and the original inhabitants of the planet – the aboriginals, as they were called. Cosmo always thought Tharn was one of the best examples of the recombination. Regal and perfectly groomed, the street theater plays put on by the populace always depicted Tharn as the handsome, kind and knowing father figure to everyone. Every mother of a male Felid in the empire told their child to be just like Tharn.

"It's all right, Cosmo." The king chuckled. "I really am sorry, in fact. They told me this was your space," he said as he glanced around at the cold stone walls in the small alcove. "Even though you can't own possessions or property, it's good to have a quiet and private spot you can go to."

"Sire, if it pleases you, I can–"

"It pleases me that you're here. As I heard, as always you are doing what you can to help."

"Sire, Master Darris must be engaged with other important activities for the princess' birthday celebrations. I am sure he will return in a moment. I – I can go get him if you'd like! He won't mind that I've given direction here."

Tharn smiled, then motioned with an open hand to the chair Cosmo had just bolted from. "Please, sit. I wanted to talk with you about that."

Cosmo quickly sat, eyes wide open and chin up as he listened. Tharn moved slightly forward and crossed his arms, then turned to lean against the table.

"Cosmo, this is your home. You are part of our everyday world. Part of our family – my family."

Cosmo blushed, fighting off a snort from the audacity of the statement's implication.

"You know what I mean," Tharn said with his own smile. "Saira is eighteen cycles old tomorrow. You've been here twelve cycles – you are what? Almost thirty now?"

"Yes, Sire."

"You made your promise at the beginning to serve me as her attendant until she reached the age of ascension. So tomorrow is the last day of that promise."

"Sire, I am eager to serve as long as you need me." Even with the king's kind words about the palace being his home, Cosmo felt a quiver of anxiety.

"Yes, I know you will. As I said, that's what I'm wanting to talk about. Master Darris and I have just had a long conversation upstairs in my chambers."

"Sire?" Cosmo was surprised. Old Darris would have been squirming in his seat if he had to stay in one place on a day like today, knowing how much was going on in the house and how many things he would have to attend to.

"He is old and tired, Cosmo, and it is time for him to retire. So..."

Cosmo waited. "So..." Cosmo repeated slowly after a moment.

Tharn just smiled and waited.

Cosmo's eyes widened as the king's visit and his words made sudden sense to him.

"Me?!"

King Tharn's smile continued through a raise of his brows.

"Sire, I– there's no way I– I'm too young!"

"What do you mean? You're thirty!"

"But–" He exclaimed, then dropped his voice to a whisper as he glanced at the doorway, beyond which were probably a score of eavesdropping kitchen staff. "House Master?"

"Cosmo, you know everyone. Everyone knows you. Everyone trusts you." Tharn laughed as he thought of it. "Hell, Cosmo, I don't think it's possible to trust anyone more than I trust you. You've cared for Saira since the day the Queen and your mother..."

He stopped and let his voice trail off. The two male Felids just looked at each other for a moment. Cosmo blinked and blew out his breath, looking down to let his eyes contemplate his porridge while his mind raced.

"Cosmo, the point of the matter is that you can do the job – you do it already, like you did a few minutes ago. Saira and I trust you and I repeat, you really are part of our family. I don't care how... improper... that sounds or if it makes you feel like I place you beyond your station. It's true."

"Sire, I appreciate that, I do." Cosmo sighed, looking up to the king's eyes quickly as he realized his impropriety of not facing the master of the Empire as he talked. But he couldn't think of what to say next.

"I guess I don't know if you've been wanting to leave, after tomorrow," Tharn mused aloud. "You certainly are free to do so."

Cosmo was surprised as he reflected on how little he had thought about it. He'd lived as the princess' caretaker and attendant for so long, and recently he had been completely tied up in arranging matters for the birthday and ascension celebrations. He'd always figured that there would have been time later on to decide what to do. Gradually.

"Sire, I will serve in whatever way you have need," Cosmo heard himself say strongly   the default and proper response for anyone speaking to a king.

"Cosmo," the king sighed and looked at the floor. His voice became very soft, and low enough that those outside the room could surely not hear it. "You have to want to do it. Sometimes I feel like... all those cycles ago... I took away your choices. I stole your life, back then, I–"

"You saved my life," Cosmo blurted. His throat caught as he realized he'd cut off the king's speech. The truth of the statement had rammed itself up out of his heart.

Tharn smiled and spoke slowly. "Cosmo, you need to think. Think about what I'm asking, and about what you want. It's very nice living here... and after tomorrow, you have more freedom and can own possessions again. But still, you have to want to be here, from now on."

The diminutive Felid put his palms on the table in front of him and leaned forward as he looked down at his porridge. In his mind was a blur – a jumble of what he'd done as the princess' attendant and his past interactions with Darris. All the people he knew in the palace. What they did, and how they did it. And himself, performing his duties and caring for Saira. But there was also a feeling that a piece was missing – something he didn't know or hadn't experienced. Yet. Something out there that was frightening but fascinating. He could feel the temptation of it dangling just out of his reach, and the bridge to that knowledge was something he realized he could start to take, if he wanted to. The day after tomorrow.

"Sire, I... I don't know what I want. I–"

He looked up, but King Tharn was gone.

two

Jalendra stood precariously, with the claws of her feet clenched and dug into the crumbling chalk of a pointed cliff outcrop. A small gray and black striped aboriginal Felid, she was slender and moved with grace and precision. Her center of gravity wavered only slightly as she stood, and with eyes closed she could focus on it – tapping it gently from moment to moment to keep herself from falling. The deadly precipice used for training was high, with razor–sharp wet rocks lining the bottom of the waterfall far below her. She welcomed the roar of the water as it went over – it helped blot out the rest of the world as she edged more and more of her athletic form into thin air.

She heard him long before he got near her – a rustle in the brush and not-soft-enough footsteps. She didn't twinge or wobble in the slightest, but her teeth clenched as she altered her pose, moving to her left foot as she took the weight off her right.

To take her mind off his approach she thought back on her rigorous training, the cycles of teaching each tiny sinew of her muscles to move the way she wanted. To only go so far, or to stop in exactly the place that they were trained to stop. With more than three quarters of her body fully over the cliff, her right foot came off the ground. Her teeth unclenched only slightly, and she let herself start a smile. Master Kem would be impressed with how far she could–

"Very nice! I remember doing that!"

Sighing, she ground her teeth together. But only for a moment – her foot came swiftly back down to let her toes grip, and she exhaled and opened her peridot green eyes. Her smile turned into to an exasperated frown as her brows bit down on her forehead.

"What?" The late morning sun illuminated a grinning Felid male leaned lazily against a tree ten feet away. His short and light sand colored fur was in stark contrast to the dark red robe he wore, and his bright eyes were striking globes of amber fire. Soft, velvety arms and legs faded to a pleasant cream color at his hands and feet. His voice showed that he was not even slightly concerned for her apparent predicament. "I used to have to do that for hours. Don't stop on my account. Master Kem would certainly want you to continue."

"Yes, he would." Jalendra's dry voice returned. She brought herself back from the edge and gradually up so that she could turn and step toward him. Her shoulders came down and her scowl faded. "If he knew you were here he would be very upset."

"You don't think he likes me?"

She looked at him sternly, tilting her head as she took a few more steps toward him. Her tail came around and seemed to form a question mark with its distinctive white tip. His tone was one that he'd probably practiced, and used to make a point.

"Kaiden, he's your father." Coming back into reality from the trance of her balance training, she became more and more aware of her surroundings. And of her clothes. Somehow, whenever she was near Kaiden she could always feel the touch of her clothes against her light covering of fur. Even though her thin shirt hung loosely off her shoulders, when he was around it seemed to actively cling to her body. The ragged trunks she wore made only the slightest of sounds as her legs traced the last few steps that led to him, but she felt every slight rub of the fabric.

"Yes, that's true," he considered, biting his lower lip and blinking his eyes as he turned them skyward in mock contemplation. "But I think we'd both agree that once he's made up his mind about someone, he–"

"Stop it." She frowned, crossing her arms over her chest. Unconsciously, her tail twitched. "You know how this makes me feel. I'm in the middle and I don't want to be. I've been in the middle since the beginning."

Kaiden held up his hands slowly in mock protest. "Easy now, easy. I'm sorry."

"It's such a male thing. I wish you two at least tried to get along – that you talked instead of just... all the glaring."

Kaiden folded his own arms over his chest and stared at her a moment before speaking. "I'm sorry. I.. I do talk. To you, anyway. He sees me and he gets too angry to talk." He looked at the dirt on the ground for a moment, before slowly tracing a scratch in it with his toe claw. "Does he talk to you? I mean – about things other than.. training stuff?"

Jalendra didn't reply. She kept her arms wrapped about herself and stood her ground, the answer to his question etched in her silence as she frowned. *You are not going to put me in the middle again.*

"He had me up here, when I was... what? Five? Doing that. He couldn't shut up. He loved telling me what I was doing wrong – his two big things: how I did things wrong, and how to kill stuff. He never talked to me about anything but training."

"I remember you being up here."

Kaiden's left eyebrow raised as he quieted and the edge of a questioning smile quivered onto his face.

"I watched you from behind the bushes over there," she said as she glanced over his left shoulder.

"Oh really? You watched me?"

He turned, and stared at the bushes she had indicated. After a moment it was clear that she was not going to answer him, so he took a long loping step in the direction of the foliage she had indicated. Then another. "Is it a secret girls–only place? Am I allowed to see?" His tail slapped the ground on each exaggerated step, making the sound of his gait comical enough to make her smile.

"Stop it." A forced look of disapproval barely covered her smile. He turned, mouth askew in a grin she knew well. The feeling of the rough cloth of her loose shirt brushing her skin was a jarring distraction as she looked across space into his eyes.

"Why are you here? Did you sneak up here to bother me, or just to make Kem angry?"

Kaiden's eyes held her face the way she imagined his hands would – softly on her cheeks and tracing up around her temples. He swallowed uncomfortably as his mouth straightened, and she could hear his sharp exhale of breath. "I'm leaving. This morning – now, really. For the north."

Jalendra remembered in a flash. His trip – his first trip as an ambassador. His first time away in a foreign land.

"To meet their princess, bring her... here," he continued, thinking that she had forgotten. "She.. she's coming to meet us. Get to know our people- "

"Yes, I remember." It was Jalendra's turn to swallow uncomfortably. Her hands came swiftly behind her back, and although she could keep a frown from her face, she could not keep her eyes steady. They wandered up and away – suddenly glancing to the trees, embarrassed to show whatever they would tell him. "I do. I remember."

"It's not for long – I mean... a day to get there, I'm there for five days, then she comes back with me. Then... then she's here for twenty. She'll be the first northern leader to ever– "

"I look forward to meeting her," Jalendra said, stopping him. "And to show her who we are as a people."

Kaiden smiled weakly.

Will you miss me? Jalendra thought.

"I... I'll be fine," Kaiden soothed. "You don't need to worry about me."

Her heart came up in her throat, yearning for different words to have been the ones he'd chosen. She forced herself to look at him. *Why is it so hard?* she asked him with her eyes as her mouth found other words. "I... I will try to remember the words you taught me. In their language – the greetings, and..."

"*Please*. *Thank You*", Kaiden spoke in the language of the northern empire, smiling. He took a deep breath and spoke to her slowly: "*Will you come to dock and say goodbye?*" He continued to smile and wait patiently, seeing if she would understand.

Jalendra thought hard. After a moment she was pretty sure she had it. "*Go to dock now?*", she queried in response.

Kaiden laughed, and switched back to their native tongue. "Haha! Fantastic! Yes, the ship – the one that's taking me. It just came in."

Jalendra smiled at his reaction, but was glad he didn't try to continue using the foreign words. She glanced around, as if expecting to see Master Kem watching her from behind a tree. As Kaiden had said, Kem seemed to delight in pointing out flaws and eagerly awaited the next mistake. She was supposed to practice her balance all morning, until the sun's position put her shadow solidly underneath her. But looking back at Kaiden she knew what she was going to do. "I'll walk you down to near the dock, but not out into the open where someone could see."

Smiling, he dipped a shoulder in a practiced ambassadorial bow, and extended an arm towards her. Changing his voice, he egged her on with an exaggerated "Your highness!"

Jalendra laughed and stepped towards him, brushing his arm aside and knocking her hip against his as he stood in his carefully practiced pose. He staggered but managed to turn to meet up with her gait as they strode towards the path down the hill. "I doubt she's going to be that aggressive," he chuckled.

"They are much more aggressive than we are."

Kaiden was quiet for only a moment as they walked down the steep incline. "They have another path from us, one they chose to suit their means and their history. They protect themselves as we protect ourselves."

"Hah! Spoken like a real ambassador. Little Kaiden's all grown up and ready to see the world!"

Kaiden smiled, but was quiet again.

"Oh, Kaiden I'm sorry. But I'm serious – you are ready to do what you've trained to do for a long time now. I can't imagine what that feels like – I'm only in the middle of my training. And Master Kem doesn't make it easy."

"No, he doesn't. But I'm proud of you for getting as far along as you are, same as you're proud of me."

She stopped, turning to him as he caught up with her. They were just on the outside of the far ring of trees that marked the ship landing area, about to step into the open sunshine. She softly blew out a shaking breath and reached out, gripping his shoulders and pulling him to her before wrapping her arms around him. She held him tight, willing him to feel what she did. Her cheeks burned and her breath fluttered as she felt his arms come around to hold her tightly against him. She could feel his breath, slow and even in his wide chest as a calm seemed to settle over both of them.

They just stood there for a minute, and Jalendra closed her eyes, soaking in how he felt. "So you will come back?" she said softly. *Will you come back to me?*

"Yes," was all he said. He pulled his face back to look at her, and for a moment she stared into black pools ringed with amber. She suddenly wasn't afraid of whatever her own eyes gave away. "In just five days. Then..."

"Yes," she sniffed once and broke the embrace, stepping backwards but letting her smile continue to hold him. "You'd better go. I – can't let anyone see me here. Kem would find out..."

He backed away until a beam of sunlight caught him, lighting up his tawny short fur. "I don't want us to hide from him," he said in a relaxed tone with a smile.

Us. She bit her bottom lip and nodded shortly.

He turned and walked down the valley towards the airship that waited for him. She watched him go and wrapped her arms around herself as her body cooled from their embrace.

thRee

The capital city of the Felid Empire was situated on the side of a mountain next to a vast crater that dropped off thousands of feet down into blackness. On the edge of the crater were the city docks floating in the air, which hosted airboats of all shapes and sizes from the Empire and from the smaller nations surrounding it. Right next to the piers were the warehouse and industrial areas and the slums – the dirty part of the city. The poorest of the population of Carnarvon lived there, mixed races in shacks and old brick buildings. Just above the slums on the lower mountainside was the sentry wall, a short but thick partition that circled the middle and upper parts of the city. All locals called it "the belt", and you lived above or below it. In the mid and upper regions, the buildings were larger and more ornate – they housed the rich, the political, and the royal. At the top of the city sprawl was the royal palace itself and its private field and airship dock, sitting on a small flat mesa up on the side of the mountain.

A long way from the palace, through thin walls Ogren could hear the noise from the slums – the calls and chatter, the regular hustle and bustle of the dirty streets. He lay in the dark in his sparse dingy room, waiting with eyes staring blankly at the ceiling. This was normal for Ogren, especially when the Human was trying to think. But the situation was certainly not normal.

Nobody's seen Jif for two days.

Jif wasn't one to be subtle – not many of the huge bear–like Ursids were. As the 'boss' of all things illicit that occurred below the belt, the more people knew about and feared Jif, the better. He normally did things out in the open – especially when he was angry about something. Just so everybody could see. And he was out every day, several times a day, walking around and checking in with his minions. Providing a presence. Ogren couldn't imagine anything that might have gone wrong or could take so much of his Boss' attention. It was as if Jif had just disappeared.

Ogren frowned at the next sound he heard – running feet, getting louder. He blinked in the dark and growled at what came next: labored breathing and fumbling at his door. The one thing Ogren had told his two runners was that appearance meant everything for the maintenance of control in the slums. From the frantic action, anyone and everyone on the street would know that something was going on. He sat up and pushed the flop of hair that adorned the left side of his head out of the way.

Tomi thrust himself through the door, wide eyes searching for Ogren in the burst of light that shone from outside. A thin and wiry Kesten, the black–and–white pelted male's thick tail thrashed around behind him as he closed the door and turned abruptly to slam his back up against it. Huffing and puffing, he gulped and in the dim light Ogren could see the thin shimmer of gloss on the Kesten's eyes.

"Better be good," Ogren rumbled. "People gonna be talking about you runnin' up to my door like this for days."

"He's dead! Jif's dead," the Kesten blurted. "All of them – all of them are dead!"

Ogren let the words hang in the air for a moment, half–expecting Tomi to correct himself, or to qualify his answer. But the heavy shuddering respirations of his runner went on uninterrupted, and Ogren himself started to feel the twinge of panic creeping up his spine.

"Did you hear me?!" Tomi erupted.

"Yeah!", Ogren bit back through the darkness. "I... I'm thinking!" He was. Fast, jumbled. Stunned. He knew he had to at least look calm. He moved his right hand up to the bald side of his head and stroked the smooth skin there. "Jif... and who else?"

"Marco and Teff. I also saw Jees and that... that thin one Jif likes... Matto."

"The five of them?! They're all.."

"Yeah! They're dead - the whole crew. Blood everywhere. Looks like quick and efficient – no message. Just slashed up. They're sitting there over at Jif's place next to the dockyard street. Been sitting there for a day or so, from what I can tell." Tomi came away from the door and sat heavily in a creaking chair.

"Doesn't make sense," Ogren growled, shaking his head. "Who... who takes out Jif?"

Tomi put his hands over his face and slid them down until they just covered his mouth. His voice was quiet and his eyes were wide as he spoke of what he had seen. "Marti found them with me, you know – Thistle's guy, the fat kid. He saw too. All that blood. Marti said... he said if you were still alive you're the only one he knew who could try..."

"ME?!! Are you crazy?! Why?"

"I'm not crazy – I told him he was! You liked Jif, you got good work from him, and you didn't wanna take over. Not your style. You're more into... background stuff."

"Damn right! But who would want to–"

Ogren's voice cut off as he heard what he thought was a footstep on the creaky floorboards outside. The door latch moved and the portal opened, illuminating Ogren and Tomi in a momentary blinding of bright light from the street.

* * *

The stinking cloth bag on his head made it hard for Ogren to breathe, so he moved as little as he could and just listened. Three. He could make out that there were three others next to the wall with him, hands tied behind their backs as they rested on their knees facing the dark room. He was pretty sure one of them was Tomi, but Ogren didn't risk saying anything. It smelt like an ale brewery, with tinges of garbage. *I'm still in the slums*, he thought to himself.

The three Felid brutes that had burst into his office hadn't roughed him up, and had barely said a word the whole time he was with them. Ogren was good with faces and even better with voices, but with the mid–day sun glaring into his darkened lair and the quickness with which they'd been able to cover his head with the sack cloth, he didn't think he'd know them if he saw them again. It didn't matter – after Jif, three felids of that size taking down someone at Ogren's level meant only one thing: somebody was cleaning house below the belt. Ogren and Tomi were well known enough to show up on anybody's list of people connected to Jif. But who were the other two guys here with them?

He didn't have to wait long. He heard a door and felt the puff of air brush past him as it opened, and inside the bag he was barely aware of illumination coming from the hallway. A shadow moved across the light, but then the door closed quickly and then there was a long silence.

"You... will all know who I am," an aristocratic Felid voice cut through the dark. While smooth at the edges, when at a low volume it had a distinctive rasp. It took Ogren a moment to sort through the jumbled mess of memories in his head, to seize on anything that matched the tone. He became frustrated that he could not remember, but then blinked, eyes widening under cover of the bag as he realized its owner. The contradiction of the particularly well–known Felid and the setting had thrown Ogren off for a moment.

"Yes," came an intonation from down the row of four figures kneeling on the floor. "Yes, we know." A Perritt from the nasal sound of the voice – thin and short humanoids, with narrow heads and long whiskers. Perritts were plentiful below the belt, and almost unheard of above it. *Fat one*, Ogren thought from the sound of its breathing. *Must be Marti, Thistle's runner.*

"Why are we here?" Ogren overtly sighed as he forced himself to sound bored. He knew the tone was dangerous, but somehow his first instinct was to make himself distinctive. Memorable. *If I'm going out here, at least somebody will remember me.*

His bag was snatched off his head. The Felid stood above him, fiery green eyes staring steadily from the blackness into his face. They danced for a moment as they considered Ogren's half–shaved head. The Human put his chin down then glanced down the line, noticing Tomi next to him but unable to make out the others in his predicament.

"Some of you are here because you have potential," the Felid said slowly. "Skills and... reputation. You are well known to my men in the slums. Mostly known for somehow never being accused of anything, but being very successful at your... whatever it is you do." He took a step down the line and snatched another bag off the next head. A greasy–faced burly Kesten that Ogren knew well – Thistle.

But he stopped before the fourth – the Perritt that Ogren could now just barely see, Marti. The thick bushy tail of the fat runner thrashed as he waited for his bag to come off.

But it didn't. The tall Felid unsheathed a long narrow knife, the elongated hilt made of smooth white bone. In his bag, Marti seized up for a moment at the sound of the knife being drawn, and then began to babble. "What? What did I do? I just found them with Tomi! I..."

Ogren could see the large Felid in front of them glance down to check and brace his footing, and then take time to position the point of his knife carefully and precisely in front of the left part of Marti's chest, in front of his heart. With only a brief pause he slowly but purposefully pushed it forwards, its sharp point penetrating through cloth and then skin.

Marti screamed. He writhed for a moment as he bucked his torso backwards from the blade, smacking his head against the wall behind them. His arms jerked and seized up at his sides but the bonds at his wrists held. The Felid calmly held the knife steady as he pushed it in further, through muscle and past bone into the beating muscle of the heart. The screams from the Perritt intensified into a garbled choke, but the Felid pushed the knife all the way in, then used his strong wrists to turn it slowly as his victim convulsed. Finally the Felid put his foot beside his knife on Marti's fat quivering chest and yanked it from him. With a final sickening gurgle the lifeless body crumpled sideways to the floor. Ogren could suddenly hear the heavy breathing of all three that remained on their knees.

"Some of you have been brought here to make a point," the Felid continued, his own breathing calm and easy despite his exertion. He casually flicked the knife towards the floor in front of them to shake thick gobs of blood from its blade.

"More than one?" Ogren forced out, barely keeping his voice steady as he had to gulp. *Keep your head. He's already decided who's going to die. If you're on the list then it doesn't matter.*

"Could be," the Felid said airily. He walked back towards Ogren in slow strides, the hide soles of his boots marking out hard steps on the wooden floor.

As he approached Ogren steeled himself and decided to go for broke – push once more. "Y–You don't get out of the p–palace much? You do this... f–for fun?"

The Felid stopped, then slowly smiled a wicked grin showing staunch white teeth. "No," he said, and paused in a comfortable silence.

His arm shot out, a perfectly placed thrusting stab of his knife that impaled Tomi as he kneeled beside Ogren. Once again directly through the heart, but this time without any time or caution to prepare. The unlucky Kesten shrieked, and gargled as he bucked forwards onto the knife. The Felid rolled his eyes distastefully and grabbed the face with his other hand and pushed hard, slamming Ogren's runner off his knife and against the back wall. Tomi's body convulsed once then went still as he died.

Ogren could feel his face burning and his heart slamming in his chest. He could not take his eyes off the blood dripping down the blade of the knife in the Felid's hands. His mind kept prompting him to speak, to say something clever – especially if this was the end. But the muscles of his mouth would not move. The only other live captive was Thistle, who also stared in wide–eyed fright at the blood–soaked blade.

"Now... either one of you want to... cry? Beg? Offer things you think I could possibly need or want? Hm?" The Felid stepped back and looked at each of them in turn. Ogren gulped but kept his head.

"Tomorrow there will be an investigation of these deaths – all of the... unfortunate... murders. I will make sure the investigation is thorough and I'm quite certain we'll find at least one perpetrator. Who will hang." He sniffed, then leaned forward to slowly wipe his knife on Tomi's clothing. With great care he moved the tip of the blade to the sheath and slid its length slowly inside. He began to pace.

"Now, you know I killed them. All my attendants know I killed them. It doesn't matter. You won't say anything – mostly because you know that if you do, you will be brought back here to make a point to others." His left hand rested calmly on the long white bone hilt that protruded from his waist.

"So, you brought us here for a s–show?" Ogren said, unable to keep his voice from wavering. He gulped and hardened his jaws, blowing his breath out his nose as he looked down to the floor.

"Yes, exactly. I am showing you what I can do. I want you to know what my limits are." He leaned in close to Ogren's face, and the Human met the green–eyed gaze that lit up the darkness. "I don't have any."

Ogren tilted his head down, dangerously looking away from the black pools in the center of the green fire. "What do you want us to do?"

"I want you to kill the princess."

Ogren's head jerked up and he turned to look with a wide eyed expression at the Kesten beside him. Thistle looked back with the same strain on his visage. Then they both slowly turned to look at the Felid.

"Quite simply, from your point of view, I just want her to be dead. I don't care how – but who did it should be a baffling mystery. Which is what you two are supposedly very good at."

Silence reigned while the two on their knees drowned in the request. The Felid began to pace again.

"It is evening now. The royal family banquet is in a couple of hours, and her birthday is tomorrow. It will be hard for you to get to her during that time, I understand. So I give you a maximum of... say... three days. In exchange for her murder before the end of that time, I will assure you the investigation leads to... someone else," he waved a hand airily. "...Whomever I decide that is."

"So we do this and you let us live?" Ogren asked.

"Yes, and I will grant you each legal commissions in my order." The Felid stopped pacing.

Ogren's eyes widened again. *A commission? Citizenship – and...*

"Freedom from the slums, a home above the belt, and a career with a future. Very nice for two resourceful street scum such as yourselves. A chance you'd never even possibly get on your own. All I ask is for your skills, and above all for your loyalty."

"There's two of us," Thistle blurted in a deep gravelly voice, clearly excited about the enormity of the proposed reward. "Why? We supposed to compete?"

"No," the Felid said calmly. He looked at both of them for a moment, then seemed to make a casual decision as he jutted his chin towards Ogren. "You. You get to kill the princess. And you..." he looked over at Thistle. "You get to kill him – if, after three days, the princess is still alive. So... I suppose you have the easier job," he smiled.

Both males looked at each other. Ogren frowned – hard. Thistle closed his eyes and breathed a sigh of relief.

"Why me? Why not him?" Ogren seethed.

"Your head looks funny. Your floppy hair on one side and... the other side without any. Very.. recognizable."

"I never understood why you wore your hair like that," Thistle said with a smile, and blew breath out his nose in a chuckle. "It sticks out."

"Mmmm," the Felid nodded in agreement. "You will have a more difficult task, and therefore you will work harder and come up with better plans to conceal yourself and whatever you do. Which is what I want."

"What if he doesn't kill me?" Ogren growled.

The Felid turned and strode to the door, opening it in a momentary gush of light. "You shouldn't worry about that. You have enough to do yourself." He stood in the portal with his back to the two would–be assassins, pausing to look over his shoulder at them. The ends of his white flowing cape twisted in the slight brush of air coming in from outside.

"In less than five days' time amid the national mourning I will quietly confer on you commissions in my order, on the steps of the hall of justice. Either that or..."

His green eyes shifted as he jutted his chin toward the two blood–soaked bodies on the ground.

four

"Kill it."

Jalendra's breath caught and she hesitated.

"Use your power," Kem's deep voice insisted. "Not your strength, not your body. Kill it now."

She reached out and gripped the wounded boar's neck, and took a breath. A moment passed in silence.

"Why do you wait? It is in pain and cannot live now."

She tried, reaching down into herself to her heart, trying to find what Kem had been talking about – the root of her power, one that he had always told her she had. The same killing power that was his specialty. His natural expertise.

She felt a warm glow inside her chest and a moment of connection to a ball of hot fire, before she whisked her mind away – scared for a moment that what she touched could burn her.

Kem reached forwards impatiently, and touched the boar only slightly on its back. The beast went rigid, eyes wide and then suddenly limp. Kem's hand quickly swept over it and closed its eyes.

"You will not eat this," Kem stated flatly in irritation. He gripped the dead beast by the back of the neck and easily lifted it with a taut muscular arm. "You did not kill it so you will not eat it."

Jalendra brought her hand back to her chest, disappointed in herself. She looked up at her master, waiting for the lesson – for the thing she had missed or needed to change for the next time. Large and stocky with charcoal gray fur, Kem was the most physically impressive aboriginal Felid that Jalendra had ever known. Even middle-aged, his rippling muscles complemented a perfectly proportioned frame with powerful extremities, wide hands and feet. Kem only ever wore two articles of clothing at most – his dark grey loincloth and a dark crimson robe. He took off his robe when he left the village and never wore it out in the jungle. The most marked difference in appearance from his son was in his eyes – Kem's deeply furrowed brow covered eyes the color of weathered bronze. They were the feature most unlike Kaiden, and the one that showed his age. The whites had been rimmed in red for as long as Jalendra could remember.

"What must I do differently, Master?"

"Nothing different. You must do more. Be more." He turned away and slung the boar over his shoulder, then started to walk long strides in the direction they had come, back towards the village. She watched his muscular back recede for only a moment before she started to follow. "You falter in the face of your power," he continued. "You are simply weak, and must become strong. Gain your power's respect by controlling it, knowing its true nature."

"How do I do this, Master? Must I kill... more?"

"Yes. Kill. You must kill as often as possible now. It doesn't matter what."

Jalendra swallowed and went quiet, and looked down to her hand. "I felt a warmth. A hot fire... inside."

"I know. A yellow fire," he stated. "It is strange to feel a color, but you will recognize it that way. I know that fire as much as you must learn it. You must master that fire. Grab it and hold it with your mind – channel it through to your prey."

"Will it burn me?"

"Yes," he answered immediately. "That fire is your destiny. You must let it consume you. And endure it. Only then can you be strong enough to use it the way it is meant to be used."

Kem moved fast. He slipped between brush and tree and over sharp rocks without the slightest hesitation. And he was perfectly silent, as if the forest wanted to hide every motion he made.

"I was afraid," she said to him as he passed out of sight behind a bush. She could hear him stop.

"We know fear. And this is like any other fear you have had – that we have trained through. You must consider your fear, but overcome it."

She came around the foliage and could see him just barely past some light branches. "What do you fear, Master?"

Kem snorted out his breath and turned to her, obviously frustrated by her question. "I fear regret. I fear a mistake I make but do not know. I fear being wrong without knowledge of it." He turned and kept moving, somehow even faster than before.

They made their way in silence for a half hour as the light in the sky started to turn to evening. Eventually they found the familiar pathway cut into a tree thicket, which led past the bottom of the waterfall that Jalendra had stood by earlier for her balance training. They were close to the village now – she could smell the new smoke from the kindling of the evening fires and hear the noise of voices just over the waterfall's dull roar.

"Master, did... did Kaiden learn to use his power? Before... before he stopped the training?"

Kem did not answer. He kept moving towards the village and did not look back at her. She trailed behind him for a moment but then with a hop she caught up. His silence continued.

"Master–"

"I do not wish to speak of Kaiden."

"Yes, Master. But you told me not to fear the questions – that between us there were none we would not ask or refuse to hear." She found the words he had taught her so many times – "the questions come, and we find the answers together."

Kem audibly growled as he walked, but seemed about to say something. It took him ten more quiet steps before he turned and stared into her face with his cold red–rimmed eyes. His voice was gravelly and held a hard tone.

"Kaiden is a failure. Simply, he is a waste of time. His mother kept him from his power. She stole his destiny. He gropes for some kind of meaning now in his life – as... a social decoration. But his true meaning – what he was meant for, is lost. He can never control the fire of his destiny. He will never have the same power that lives in you."

She blinked at him for a moment – it was more than she'd ever heard him say about his son, and she struggled to process it. She knew Kaiden's mother had died a long time ago, at the same time Kaiden had stopped training altogether. Her mind pressed her with more questions, but she knew she had already gone further than Kem was comfortable. She bowed her head in appreciation for his answer, and remained silent.

He huffed out a breath, and looked past her back the way they had come. The sun was lower in the sky but Zefphyr's twin moons could still be seen over the hillside. Nodding slightly to himself, his voice changed and he spoke to her gruffly – as he did when he was commanding her to train harder. "You will not be a failure. Find your power. Now. Go back the way we came. Find your power and use it the way it is intended, and you will find the path to your destiny." He turned abruptly away from her and stomped towards the village, but called back in a stern tone: "Do not return until you have done so."

Jalendra stood for a moment staring at her master as he walked away, a nervous fear in her stomach. She had barely touched the feeling when they'd killed the boar. What if she couldn't get it back again? Couldn't control it? It would burn her – Kem had told her it would. How could she possibly overcome her body's instincts? She sighed and turned around, heading slowly back towards the hunting grounds.

five

Cosmo sighed, eyes turning to the ceiling as he waited.

"One more minute. I'm almost ready," the teen female voice assured.

One more minute.

One more minute.

One more minute.

To pass the time Cosmo adjusted the belt of his black robe, then flicked off two pieces of lint that had found their way onto his shoulder. His distinctive black and white color added to the uniformity of his robe, and he always managed to find anything that even slightly affected his appearance. He brushed down his front, then removed his spectacles to blow off a hair or two that had settled across the thin lenses. He squinted at them and then replaced them on his face, scrunching his nose once to let the metal bridge settle. Then he sighed loudly.

One more minute.

"Princess, we literally have only one minute before the banquet is to start. Your father and uncle will both be very unhappy with me if we appear late."

"Oh Cosmo, be patient. You're always like this."

"Yes, I've always been like this. I have this really strange unnatural power of knowing how your father will react to things."

Saira emitted an exaggerated teenage sigh from behind the curtain. Cosmo ignored it and looked around the room, assessing the furniture and the walls, the ceiling. He thought about how much bigger the palace was than this one room. It was overwhelming for him to even consider being in charge of it all. He moved to the tower window to look out through the dim late evening light at the rest of the buildings. He tried to estimate the number of floors, rooms, furniture, things. The people.

"You are always pushing me to get to the next thing and the next, but you do it with this irritated... exhaustion in your voice. Maybe that's it. Maybe you're tired of me..." the princess trailed off in a teasing tone.

Cosmo didn't answer her as both his eyes and his mind glazed over at the enormity of the responsibility that the king had offered him. How could it possibly be conceived that he could handle it all?

Saira's voice turned to a whining forced hurt at his silence. "You don't want to be my friend anymore?"

"Do I want to be your friend any more..." he mumbled aimlessly as he snapped out of it, closing his eyes to concentrate. He crossed his arms and lowered his chin to his chest. His ears were too large for his stature, and with his head down the snowy white cravat at his neck made him appear as frustrated as he felt.

"Cosmo?"

"I'm sorry– I... I was thinking."

"About what?"

Cosmo sighed. "Your father talked to me this morning about–" He cut himself off as his mind pulsed another warning about the time. "It– it doesn't matter. We can talk about it later. Please hurry."

She came out from behind the dressing curtain, and Cosmo had to blink in amazement at her beauty. The white dress she wore was designed to echo the elegant lines of the snow lilies found in the royal garden, the bodice form–fitting with a laced back. Sleeves started at the outside of her shoulders and ended right above her elbows. The skirt skimmed over her hips and down her thighs, then flared out just above her knees into a trumpet bell. Made of heavy satin, it was pure and bright and shimmered even in the low light of the room.

She came forward and turned in front of him, smiling as she brushed her hair back over one shoulder. He noted her signature scent – a soft lilac he'd gotten used to over the cycles. "Do me up?" she asked politely.

"I will, but then we go right away. No more dilly–dallying."

He started to tie her gown, struggling with the thin slippery tendrils that made up the lacings at the back. After two attempts of straightening and loosening, he huffed out a frustrated sigh and reached around to grab under the front of her chest, pulling her bosom firmly upwards.

"Oh my word, Cosmo," she said, bringing a hand to her mouth to stifle a faked gasp. "So forward with your improper affections!"

"Oh, save it," he bluntly retorted with a huff. "Just hold them up like this for a second will you?"

She did and he used both his hands to clinch ties at the back, nimble fingers working to get the bows into their proper place. "I see everything you've got regularly and believe me it's not something I pine for more of."

"You don't think I'm pretty?"

He blinked his eyes slowly and sighed as he withdrew his hands and patted her lightly on the back, signaling he was finished. She turned to him and he straightened out her front by gripping the sides of her dress at the waist.

"You're the most beautiful girl I've ever seen, okay? Trust me. Nobody else comes close." He smiled quickly, then turned away and started for the door. "But I can't help it," he shrugged. "Reason I got this job in the first place. I'm not into girls – never have been. Not interesting to me."

"So I'm pretty but I'm boring?"

Cosmo sighed loudly, but he wasn't going to bite. They walked from the doorway of her chambers through to his own, which served as a safety buffer from the rest of the world. Crossing the floor of his simple, sparsely adorned room, they stopped at the entrance to the tower steps that led downwards. Cosmo opened the door and stood waiting for Saira in silence, eyes stiffly rolled skyward.

The princess took her time as she followed his path, making a coy, questioning face to accentuate the fact that he had not answered her question. "Hmmm?" she intoned as she stopped beside him and gave a tilt of her head.

"I have decided that I am not talking to you anymore," he said without breaking his eye roll.

She broke into a grin and walked past him out the door and softly toed down the steps. "Yes, you are."

"No, I'm not."

"Yes, you are."

"No, I'm not."

Down the stairs of the darkened tower they went, through the guard stations and into the wide empty front hallway of the palace.

"Nobody's here?" Saira looked around, questioningly.

"No, nobody's here. They're all at your banquet – you know, the one that I've been trying to get you to go to for the past half mark?"

"You should have told me we were late."

Cosmo growled in exasperation and continued down the hallway towards the banquet hall. Saira had to move quickly, her dress rustling as she hurried to keep step with him.

"Ooh – is the ambassador from the prime clan here yet?" Saira queried. The southern aboriginals organized in clans, composed in a hierarchy of villages. While each village was wholly independent and inter-village quarrels did occur, a clan was an extended family. The varied genetically modified species that lived in the Felid Empire called the largest and most well-known of these families the prime clan.

"No, his ship gets in very late tonight, tomorrow morning really. He'll see all the birthday celebrations – you can meet him then, after you have sobered up. Tonight it's just the usual trove of family and invited guests. A couple of new boys for you to meet as well."

"I promise to behave."

"Hah! Right. Like last time?"

"Last time didn't count. He was cute."

"Even I agree he was cute. But if I wasn't there I'm sure you would have snuck off with him to some deserted corner of the castle, or worse, tried to take him all the way to your room."

"I wouldn't do that!" Saira protested. "You're just jealous I saw him first! He was fun."

"Maybe. But he was... stupid."

"Yes," she sighed and made a half frown as she remembered. "He was pretty dumb."

They approached the large wooden doors of the main hall and could hear the sound of talk and laughter. Cosmo stopped her, putting himself between the door and his charge. The white tips of his hands were bright in the light of the hallway, and the subtle striping in his black coat made him appear much older than he actually was. He looked into her face with pleading eyes. "Seriously now. Can we be a little less... flirty... this evening?"

"Oh Cosmo. Sure I flirt – aggressively sometimes. Isn't that normal for someone my age? So far I've only had what.. two possible real suitors?" She hated the word. "You followed around and loomed over both of those! And if any boy I was with – even for fun – took a fertility pill both you and I could smell it on them by the time they're potent. So even if I was a floozy I can't get pregnant unless I want to. As long as they're healthy and clean what's the problem of... playing?"

"You're right that the... aggressive flirting... as you put it, is natural and I don't really care about it. And I'm very happy the Masters controlled breeding the way they did. I just don't want you to get hurt. We need to find you someone gentle and kind, strong but thoughtful. If he's good looking that's a bonus."

"What if a boy like that is here tonight? What if he's cute?"

"Then... you and I will have a serious conversation. But for a princess I think you're already more experienced than you should be."

She sighed again, grudgingly, but nodded. "Ok. We'll have a serious conversation. Quickly. Expeditiously. Maybe... nonverbally."

Cosmo sighed yet again and pushed open the door behind him. It swung open to reveal a room full of white–garbed male and female felids, attended to by an abundant flock of black–robed servants. A cheer and raised glasses went up as Saira came down the two short steps into the sunken room and graciously performed a deep curtsy for the revelers. Cosmo faded into the background, but kept his eyes on her.

King Tharn stood up from his seat, his face a study in pride. "My dearest love," he proclaimed, eyes fixed lovingly on his daughter. "Happy Birthday!"

Another cheer from the gathered guests, and Saira approached her father with a smile. As she did so, Cosmo could see the king's eyes find him in the backdrop at the edge of the room. Given the barest of nods as a silent thank–you, Cosmo felt a warmth of pride in his chest and dipped his own chin slowly to return the greeting. The king smiled and returned his eyes to his daughter.

"Eighteen!" Saira exclaimed in excitement, raising her brows as if she herself was shocked to have reached the milestone. She came forward and leaned to kiss her father on his cheek.

"My dear, you look lovely." He turned to look to his left. "Don't you think so, Jasper?"

Lord Jasper, brother and baron to the king, stood beside him. Saira's uncle was dressed almost exactly the same as the king, but even though they were also white his robes were noticeably less bright, and he wore a green sash prominently around his waist. Also in stark contrast was the orange color of his fur and skin, and the dark black that rimmed his eyes and ears. Uncharacteristic for a Felid, the jet–black hair on the back of his head was very long, and braided into a ponytail that extended down the middle of his back. Jasper nodded once with a smile towards Tharn, then turned to face Saira and bowed deeply. He turned to pick up two silver goblets from the table beside him, each of his hands carefully cupping the ornate silver bowl at the top of a jeweled stem. Extending one arm towards Saira, he smiled broadly as he offered her one. She took it and held it out to the attendant who stepped up with a full bottle of wine.

"A toast to the loveliest future queen in the history of the Empire." Jasper's strong voice filled the room, loud enough for everyone to hear. "Please – all fill your glasses."

Cosmo watched as Saira's goblet was filled and she raised it quickly towards her lips. But her father waved down her arm. "Ah, ah! First toast is for you, love. Tradition speaks that afterwards you must tell us how it feels to be eighteen, and then if you wish you may toast us...", he chuckled. "And if I know you, you will many times."

She brought down the goblet and nodded her head, calmly waiting. There was silence as the rest in the hall had their first drink – most of them draining their entire glasses. Jasper finished his and gently nodded to Saira then to King Tharn.

"Father, I am very happy to be your daughter and be so fortunate of family, health, and friends." She turned to the room and looked around for Cosmo, finding his eyes as he stood in the shadows. "My only birthday wish is long life for us all, and–"

Jasper suddenly choked, doubling over forwards and dropping his empty goblet. A mouthful of wine burst from his mouth as he sunk to his knees. There was a collective gasp from the crowd, and two guards on either side of the king jumped forward to put themselves between him and the sudden fracas. Saira stepped back in surprise, also dropping her goblet on the floor. Then Jasper started to violently vomit – great heaving spews of half–digested food. His attendants flocked to him as guards also surrounded the princess, pushing her backwards towards the door. For a moment Cosmo stood his ground, wide eyes unable to leave Jasper as the Felid fought to scream through regurgitation that blocked his windpipe and convulsions that rocked through his body. He very quickly began to vomit blood.

Cosmo rushed and pushed hard past revelers towards the entrance to the room that Saira had been dragged from, catching sight of her glassy eyes and shocked face as she was roughly hustled into the palace. He could hear her start to cry as they whisked her past the guard posts and back up the stairs to her room. In the pit of his stomach he felt two things – bewilderment at what had just happened, and deep fear in his stomach that whatever Jasper had eaten or drunk had been meant for Saira.

The guards dragged Saira through Cosmo's room into her own and tried to put her on her bed, but she sank to the floor in front of it. A tall thin male in apothecary robes surged through the retreating troops and grabbed at her face, looking into her eyes then at her hands, before forcing her mouth open to look at her tongue and to swipe a finger over it. Cosmo finally caught up to them.

"Hey, easy! Easy! She's fine. Calm down – you're scaring her! What is wrong with you?!"

"Mister Cosmo, I don't know if you noticed but there has been an attack on the Royal Family," the apothecary angrily snapped. "The castle is locked down and I have been told by Captain Valaria to immediately assess the princess' health and report to her. The princess is not to leave her quarters until you hear from the captain or the king directly, in person." The male abruptly turned and bustled out of the room, leaving a sobbing Saira at the foot of her bed.

"Wha.. what just happened?" Saira choked, having trouble breathing through her cries. "Uncle Jasper – he.. is he..?"

Cosmo knelt next to her, pulling her forward against his chest to calm her down. "I don't know. I– I don't know. He was poisoned – I'm pretty sure of it. You– you're ok, right? You feeling ok?"

She nodded, unable to speak as she struggled to breathe through the wracking cries that seized her chest. But she gripped his arms and held herself to him. "Cosmo – was that for me? Was that supposed to happen to me? If... if I drank would–"

"I don't know. We'll never know – you dropped your goblet so we can't test that wine. But your father didn't get sick, and he drank. Others drank. Maybe it was the goblet. There were two goblets that Jasper had. Whoever gave them to him could have poisoned them. But I don't know."

"What do we do, Cosmo?! It's my birthday tomorrow – the celebrations. I'm supposed to be out in the open, eating and drinking all day with the people. What do I do? Why would somebody want to hurt me?"

"Shh. Shhh... nobody's trying to hurt you. All the people – everybody loves you. Maybe somebody is mad at your Uncle Jasper... I don't know. But we can't assume they're after you."

"We have to," King Tharn stated flatly from the doorway.

"Oh, father!" Saira blurted, jumping up from the floor out of Cosmo's arms to rush to her father. She started to cry again as she sank into his white robes. His worried face reflected Cosmo's own as the two males looked at each other with stoic concern.

"Father, is... is Uncle Jasper..?"

"He's alive, but struggling. They stopped the progression of the poison, got him to stop vomiting and take water. But he's still having convulsions and can't talk."

"Oh my goodness – why?! Why would someone do this?"

"We don't know. Jasper has enemies, but none so bold or well-connected as to attack him in the palace. The only other possibility is that the poison that Jasper received was meant for someone else."

"Who?" Saira blurted. She stared into his face and he swallowed with a heavy sigh. The answer was clear.

"I can't believe that," Cosmo muttered, crossing his arms and looking down at the floor in frustration. "Everyone loves her – the people can't wait to see her every time we go out, and all she does outside the castle is help people in need. So who? She's socially important – but immature and relatively powerless. Not even barely political yet. What does anyone gain by killing her now?"

"I'm right here, Cosmo!" Saira bit out angrily, moving away from her father to plunk down on her bed. She grabbed her pillow and hugged it to herself. "Don't talk about me like I'm not!"

Cosmo sighed. "Sire, the celebrations tomorrow are not a good idea."

"I agree," Tharn said. "They are cancelled."

"What?!" Saira exclaimed, tears coming to her eyes again. "After days and days of everyone getting ready for them? The children! The children's parade... I promised some of them personally that I would walk with them. And the fireworks... the fair?"

"Cancelled! I won't risk your life by putting you out where you're an easy target. And given where we were and who was allowed to be present, the only people we can certainly rule out as the attackers are we three and Jasper."

"What about the southern ambassador?" Cosmo queried.

"He's not even here yet! There's no way for him to even know anyone here, and it wouldn't make any sense. You think he had something to do with this?"

"No... But... he does get here in less than two marks. After this, can we even protect him properly?"

"Probably not. Not if we can't protect ourselves." The king swore and paced, then sat down heavily on the end of the bed. "This is a disaster."

All three sat in silence for minutes, Saira fighting hard to stifle her tears.

"We'll turn him around and you'll go with him," the king stated flatly. Both Cosmo and Saira turned their heads slowly to face Tharn, trying to make sense of his plan. The king's eyes were defocused as details settled in his mind.

"The aboriginals are expecting you to go back with the ambassador – we're just sending you a little early. It will be as if we just sent the ambassador home, which we would have done anyway. Cosmo, you'll go with her, at least until she gets there. Nobody else will know."

"What?!" Cosmo blurted. "Me?! I can't go on a ship! Leave the city?! I don't want–"

"I can't go!" Saira exclaimed. "I'm not ready!"

The king's eyes blinked as he finalized the decision in his mind. "You're as ready as you need to be. And Cosmo, tomorrow is your last day as her attendant, but are you going to leave her, and me, when we need you the most?"

Cosmo's brows came down and his head tilted forwards in consternation. *The South? Me?* He couldn't even imagine wanting to go on such a trip.

"Father, it's the middle of the night now! You have to at least give us a day or so to get ready!" Saira continued her protestations. "I don't have any suitable clothes, gear, anything."

"My word is final," the king said as he nodded to himself. "You have to go right away before anyone can follow you. You leave tonight when the ship gets here – pack whatever you can, and don't tell a soul if you can help it. I'm sorry my love, but this is best to protect you until we figure out what is going on and who was the target."

Saira sniffed, her eyes welling up again.

"I'm so sorry my love. The palace should be the safest place in the kingdom. The only other place I'd trust with people knowing where you are is on board the Castegeir. And Captain Archer's... a thousand kilometers away right now, at least."

Cosmo put his fingers to his forehead for a moment, then looked up at the king.

"Do your job," Tharn said sternly to Cosmo. "Protect our family. There is no one else I can trust right now."

SIX

Jalendra trekked for hours into the dark wilderness until she started to hear noises of the animals skittering away as she moved. Her footfalls became quieter, her eyes widened and her ears came up. Eventually she stopped, coming up to a large ironwood tree and crouching down at its base.

For a long time she crouched perfectly still in shadow of the light from the moons, keenly aware of every nuance that came to all her senses. She searched for the motion of a boar, or a bird, or any other animal of substance that she knew Kem would agree was a challenge. Her muscles ached from being forced to stay in the same place for so long. *This isn't working,* she finally thought. *I've picked the wrong spot.* It happened sometimes even when she hunted with Kem, and she didn't dwell on it. She stood to stretch and take a deep breath, but stopped instantly halfway to standing.

It was coming towards her. Something smaller than the boar she and Kem had found earlier, but still with weight to displace the foliage. She slowly sank back down to a crouch and controlled her breathing. Her eyes stretched wide. The tiny hairs in her ears let her test the direction of the wind, and she confirmed to herself that she was not giving away her position by her scent. *An easy kill,* she thought to herself. *Easy for my body.* But what about her mind?

All female felids – even after genetic manipulation by the Masters – had single primary talons in each of their hands. Between the index and middle fingers a sharp point protruded through a rough patch of thick, tough folded skin. Jalendra could extend each of her talons almost two inches, using the natural razor–sharp edges to fight or hunt. She closed her hands into fists and let the animal instinct inside her start to take over. As each of her talons extended she felt the growing rush of her heartbeat and listened intently for sounds from her prey.

She kept reassessing its size, and was disappointed when it seemed smaller and smaller to her as it approached. She wished it had been something larger, more of a challenge. Something more impressive to overcome. She considered letting it go, but her heartbeat was surging already, pushing her to act.

The skrit rat never saw her or smelled her. Indeed, it hardly knew what had happened before it was in the vicelike grip of her right hand, with the perfect point of her left talon pressed across its throat. It went crazy – struggling and scratching with its back legs, writhing its body and bucking its back as it fought to get free.

Jalendra resisted the natural urge to simply slash the throat or stab the chest with her outstretched talon. She seethed breath at her own restraint – pushing back against her instinct and physical training to put her mind to the front. To let her power kill the creature. Her mind alone.

The skrit spasmed and scratched at her, eyes wide as it fought to breathe and to try to get one of its claws under her grip. She held firm and closed her own eyes, separating herself from its manic constrictions, to focus her mind inward and downward.

The warm glow came back again, and the sense of a ball of fire burning on itself. As Kem had said, she had the strange sensation of feeling the color, the yellowness of the burning core. As it had been with the boar she was scared for a moment, but this time stopped herself against the pull back towards the physical fight – the scratching twisting clawing world outside herself.

She reached down, purposefully deeper, and pushed aside her fear to connect to the color in the flames. The warmth seized her and she felt it, connected to it and let it flow into her. A burst of electric power surged in her mind as she felt the knowledge she could dominate the yellow fire. Control it and wield it as she knew she could any muscle. She did – surprised at the ease of routing it from her mind into and through her body.

But as she did a sickening nausea surged in her gut, and it was as if icy claws pierced and seared across the back of her neck. She felt the heat and the pain of the yellow flames, but only for a moment. Only a lick of the power brushed up through the connection.

The skrit went limp in her grasp. She felt the change and was surprised by the sudden cease in the struggle. She flicked open her eyes.

It was dead.

Almost instantly she could feel its lifelessness. Bleak empty lifelessness, cold as a wilted flower. But linked to her hand. Her hand linked to her arm, and her arm to her chest. Through to her heart. Charred cold embers. The fire had done its job and vanished.

She dropped the skrit, frightened by the connection to the new type of cold she hadn't felt before. The body fell to the ground in a sprawled lump, wide eyes illuminated in the blue light from the twin moons. She stared at it and grimaced against the remains of nausea that had surprised her. She shut her eyes to force it out of her mind, but the feeling inside her did not drop away. The core of cold remained in her body, like a rod of ice – all parts of her body that she had used to channel the fire had been cauterized.

She then felt two things in quick succession.

The first was a deep yearning to have the yellow fire back – to know and use the feeling of mastery that her instinct recognized. To make the fire fill her up and warm the cold space where she had channeled its flames – where it was supposed to be. The euphoria of connecting to her destiny.

The second feeling was a washing wave of shame. Her cheeks burned and a dizzying sickness radiated from her stomach as she thought of wanting – needing – to feel and control death. As she had felt the color of the yellow in the flames, she knew the black purpose that was at their core.

She left the skrit where it had fallen, overwhelmed by disgust in the thought of touching it again.

seven

Life in Carnarvon was always busy, and always noisy. At all hours out in the streets the many members of the different races plied their wares, advertised services from the mundane to the bawdy, and even entertained for handouts if they had no other skills. Most of the street people were completely uneducated – having abandoned the schools as soon as they could work to bring in money for themselves and their families.

Hooded and cloaked, Cosmo and Saira made their way in the still–dark of early morning through the back alleys of the slums with their sole escort – the captain of the guard, Valaria. They were stopped abruptly here and there by the captain so she could watch for anyone who might be following them, and were randomly hushed so that she could listen.

Cosmo was on edge and hated every moment of the journey. He clutched his robe close to his body, one arm wrapped around his small case – the only thing he had been able to find for their impromptu trip. *A spare set of glasses, two loincloths and a formal robe*, he thought. *I hope they know how to wash clothes.* He swallowed hard. *And don't run around naked.*

The sum total of travel he had ever done in his life was to the royal family's summer retreat in the west, far enough away for him to dread the journey and yearn for their return to the comforts and consistency of the palace. He looked out at the groups of people moving about the barely–lit thoroughfare and then around at the alley they stood in, blowing air out his nose to try to avoid the stink.

"How far now?" Saira queried. She at least had been able to find suitable clothing – a brown tunic, pants and a forest green hooded cape. The tunic skimmed her body and ended near the top of her thighs under which the close–fitting pants became visible. Leather greaves completed the protection for her legs, bound above soft suede ankle boots. Her cape was clasped closed around her neck and flowed down her back to mid–calf, but was open enough to show her wide leather belt.

"Almost there, your highness," Valaria responded. They were heading toward the city's base, where the cliff edge of the crater housed a huge array of floating airships. "Two blocks or so and we'll be at the docks. From there I must leave you to find your way. If I am seen someone will easily figure out where you have gone."

"Why didn't the king send someone else with us, then?" Cosmo growled. "You think I know my way around here? You think she does?"

Valaria turned. The captain was an exceptionally tall female Felid, with a strikingly angular face and closely cropped hair. Her dark gray guard's uniform contrasted with her pure white coloring, making her recognizable in almost any environment. "I'm sorry, Mister Cosmo. But the king trusts no–one else after the attack." She swallowed hard and sighed. "He even interrogated me before we left."

"Valaria!" Saira barked in surprise. She grabbed Valaria by the lapel to look into her eyes. "I trust you with my life. You know that. My father is just scared and is being careful. You don't deserve suspicion." The captain was silent for a moment as she returned the stare, but then broke her gaze and nodded curtly in agreement.

"What are we supposed to do on our own?" Cosmo injected. "You don't think I'll be out of place without you, wandering about asking what ship the ambassador is coming in on?"

"Sir, if I am correct you seldom venture out of the castle. Nobody around here should know you. She, on the other hand..." her voice trailed off as she turned back to address the princess. "Your highness, you must stay out of sight. Wait until Mister Cosmo has spoken with the captain, then go aboard the ship in the way that he tells you. It will not be the normal way."

Valaria paused for breath, looking around the corner out into the street again. "The ship is called the *Daedalus* – it's a federated transport and should be safe, once you get on board. I trust the captain and have spoken to him over a secure comm connection. He knows to let you aboard the ship with no questions asked, and where to take you. Are you ready to move the last two blocks?"

"I am," Saira said with wide eyes. She looked past Valaria at the street. Cosmo simply grunted and pushed his spectacles up his nose. The three of them quickly moved out down the alleyway, across the street and past the back of a tavern, where a bright patch of light came from an open door. Valaria darted past the door, then turned quickly back to beckon to them. As they both came across the illuminated area, Cosmo instinctively turned his head to glance through the opening. He spied a face – a nondescript dirty furred face looking straight back at him in the moment he crossed the lit threshold of the door. He felt a pang of guilt in his gut and clenched his teeth, but continued on after Valaria and the princess down another alley and around a corner. The guard captain stopped and pulled them both close to her, hands on their shoulders.

"Did anyone see you? Word travels fast below the belt. Faster than you can imagine."

Cosmo was quiet for a moment, not wanting to admit that he'd been clearly seen.

"Not me," Saira said. "Cosmo?"

"Nobody knows me," Cosmo bit out, refusing to look into Valaria's eyes. "You said it yourself. Why would it matter?"

Valaria was quiet, staring at him for a moment.

"It's all right, captain," Saira said softly. She raised her hand and placed it firmly on top of hers. "Sending me away secretly is silly, but whatever my father's ridiculous suspicions, he was right to trust you. You did your job well – nobody saw us and we're here. Return to the castle and tell him we got away safely." The princess smiled at her, then turned to Cosmo, who clutched his case and looked crossly at the ground. "Ready?"

"No," he grumbled sarcastically.

She curled her arm around his back and pulled him across the lit street to the fence that ran along the edge of the docks. Ten feet away was the main entrance, and they managed to cross the distance and move through without any sign they'd been noticed. Cosmo looked back at where they had stood and saw that Valaria was gone.

"Come on, Cosmo. You've got to find this ship."

"She would have been better at this," Cosmo continued to grumble as they moved along the darkened planks next to the moored ships. "Your father decided to trust her, so why couldn't she go?"

"Everybody in the kingdom knows Valaria, Cosmo," Saira said as she stopped and looked about at the mass of ships that seemed to be moored randomly about them. "She goes somewhere and people notice – they remember. Please stop whining."

Cosmo bristled. Even though he could see she was tentative, there was a sparkle in her eyes and a snap in her movements from the submersion into a new environment. "You seem as though you're actually enjoying this," he grumbled.

"Yes, I am. Now. It's happening, so... it's new. I'm enjoying it. I like new things. Like... surprises and sneaking around in the dark."

Cosmo groaned and glanced left and right under his drawn brows. "Oh to be a teenager again. You're excited but you don't know where you're going or what you're doing."

"No, I don't. So I need you. Go ask someone the way to the *Daedalus*."

"Can't we just walk around for a while and see if we can find it?"

Saira's brows hunched and for a moment she stared at him exactly the way he stared at her. He snorted and put down his case at her feet, then turned to walk cautiously towards a lighted kiosk half a dock–length away.

Coming up to the light, he saw a thin Human dock worker slumped in a chair, eyes closed with a bottle in his lap. Cosmo cleared his throat and knocked lightly on the edge of the doorway. "Uh – ahem. Sir?"

"Mmmph." The Human barely moved his mouth but nothing else.

"The.. uh.. *Daedalus*. It's...?"

"Two Seven."

"Uh... interesting. Yes. Hm. What... what does that mean?"

The man's head came forward and he opened his eyes, blearily blinking at Cosmo for a second. "Pier Two, Slot Seven."

"Ah. Pier two. I.. I uh – and where are we now?"

"Three Two."

"Ah, I see three–two. Okay. So–"

"Don't get down here much, do you?" The man sniggered, looking amusedly at Cosmo's black servant's robes. "Nice dress you're wearing. Don't see many of those."

Cosmo licked his lips nervously, but the Human jutted out his chin in the direction that Cosmo had come from. "Next pier that way."

"Excellent. Thank you fine sir. Good evening."

Cosmo bowed and withdrew quickly, away from the doorway and the light, and moved off back towards where he had left the princess. She was exactly as he had left her, and had not even touched his case. He bent over and picked it up. "Two Seven. That way."

"Two seven? What does that mean?"

"Pier two, slot seven," Cosmo said impatiently with an audible tsk. "We're at three two. Come come, basic stuff."

They moved along and down pier two, walking a quarter of a mile out from the cliff edge at the bottom of the city. They passed a few other motley figures on the way that carried goods from the ships, but were not stopped or even overtly noticed. They quickly drew upon a well–lit slot where a ship was being unloaded, and slowed to a stop just out of the bright halos of illumination.

"This must be it," Cosmo said as he turned and put his case at the princess' feet. "Let me go and make sure," he said with a slight smile as he confidently pushed his spectacles up his nose.

"You seem as though you're actually enjoying this," Saira deadpanned back at him.

"I'm not. I hate new things," he said slyly, turning away. "Like... surprises and sneaking around in the dark."

Cosmo came alongside the ship to the mid–deck area, walking directly towards the gang–plank. But as he walked casually past a large Mantarian dock worker, a shout went out and he froze. The dock worker reached forwards and gruffly pulled Cosmo towards him – as a huge crate came down and landed in the spot where the thin Felid had just been standing. "Watch your step, guy," was all the Mantarian said as he turned to start to work on the rigging of the crate.

Cosmo stepped back and blinked, then gingerly made his way the rest of the distance to the gang plank. Looking up it he saw a stout long–faced Impalan dressed in a thick jacket and broad hat staring back at him. "*Daedalus?*" Cosmo queried.

"You got it. Captain Fasil at yer service," the male said loudly and confidently. "Ye looking for passage?" As he spoke he widened his eyes and nodded at Cosmo, coaxing a quick and simple answer.

"Uh, uh yes. Just... just me. And... uh my.. some things I brought."

"Good. We just touched in but we're loadin' and leavin' in a split." He stood waiting for Cosmo to say or do something, but his patience quickly ran out. "Why don't ye come up here and I'll take yer money?"

Cosmo looked openly back the way towards where he knew Saira was hiding, then realized how stupid it was to directly point out to anyone watching exactly where she was. He turned 90 degrees to emphasize looking away from her, and felt instantly even more idiotic. He sighed and looked down at the boards of the dock, then started trudging up the gang plank towards the captain.

When he reached the top of the plank at the edge of the ship, the captain suddenly held up an open palm to stop him. Cosmo blinked and stared, suddenly worried. As he stared a heavy thick rope suddenly dropped past his gaze onto the deck between himself and the captain, thudding onto the dock with a vibration that shook through Cosmo's feet.

The captain's open hand quickly rotated and he beckoned the Felid forward. "Gotta watch them ropes," he chuckled. "They go up 'n down right quick and they're huge buggers. C'n squish ya or get under ya and throw ya inta the air if yer not watchin' out."

"Captain, sir," he proclaimed loudly so that others could hear him clearly. "I wish to travel, by myself, to–"

The captain waved him silent with a patting of his hand in the air. "Sssh – sshh. It's ok," he said quietly. "I know who ye are. Where's the uh... young Miss... at?"

Cosmo cocked a brow, unsure at how direct an answer he should give. "She's safe," he whispered back "Nearby. How is she to get aboard?"

The captain beckoned to a shorter Impalan deckhand, and simply pointed to Cosmo while looking at her. "Miss Stan here will go with ye te get – uh.. yer things. Then ye come back up here and go into that 'lil hole of a room over there..." he cast an arm towards a tiny portal in the side of the ship's forecastle. "We'll make sure yer... belongings... make it in there. After that we can link ye up with yer foreign companion."

"Foreign compa– oh. Oh yes. Our friend from the south. Excellent – I mean. Uh, aye–aye, captain." He saluted clumsily and turned to head down the gangplank. The captain rolled his eyes and motioned for Miss Stan to follow Cosmo.

In less than ten minutes Cosmo was back aboard inside the tiny room with both his and Saira's travel belongings. Saira herself had never entered the light or come up the gangplank – moments after taking Miss Stan to meet up with her, the two females had disappeared into the shadows.

He sat nervously and waited, listening to the creaking and banging sounds on the ship, as well as the curious calls from the deckhands as they worked to prepare to leave the docks. He had just closed his eyes to concentrate on calming his nerves when a trapdoor in the floor popped open, startling him. Saira stuck her head through with a smile.

"Boo!" she chuckled. "We're here. We made it. I don't think anybody saw me get on. Miss Stan is nice – doesn't talk much, but nice."

"Well," Cosmo started in a condescending tone. "I'm so glad you're making new friends. Did you tell her our whole plan?"

"Oh, Cosmo. She got on the ship with me and she's not getting off. We're about to leave but... she said nobody has told the ambassador yet. They've just delayed him leaving. He still thinks he's getting off."

"What?!" Cosmo exclaimed. "What do you mean nobody's told him?"

She shrugged. "I don't know. She said they gave him some story about paperwork and he's waiting in the guest quarters. You need to tell him what's going on."

"What – is that my job? Why is that my job? You're the royalty! You're supposed to be the one who... meets people and goes places. I don't know how to talk to a foreign ambassador!"

"I can't leave here!" Saira hissed, bringing up a single index finger to her mouth to ask him to lower his voice. "Not while we're still at the dock, anyway. And we can't invite him into this little hole. Won't that look a bit strange to anyone who's watching? He's just an ambassador, Cosmo. He's not a king and it's his job to not get easily offended."

Frustrated, Cosmo rushed to stand and banged his head on the low roof of the compartment they were in. He seethed and rubbed the crown of his head, sighing as he opened the door and stepped out onto the deck. Straightening his robe he walked across the deck towards the captain, but halfway the Impalan simply pointed towards the door of a cabin on the back part of the ship. Adjusting his path Cosmo moved smoothly towards the door and then knocked gently upon it.

The door drew open and the ambassador appeared in the entrance, a calm smile on his face. "Ah – It brings me happiness to greet you, noble," the young southerner said with a thick accent. It looked like effort, but he seemed happy to get to use the language he had obviously practiced, and his tail swished behind him in a gentle sway. "I am ambassador. Kaiden. I have waited. I wish to leave the ship. We will enter your capital city now?"

Oh crap. Cosmo stared into Kaiden's face as his mind flicked to Saira. *He's cute.* He took a breath and pushed through to explain the situation. "Yeah, about that. Uh... slight change of plans. I am not noble. I am her attendant."

"Attendant? Ah..." Kaiden waited for Cosmo to say more, but when nothing came he raised his eyebrows and looked to the deckhands securing the cargo. He frowned. "I do not understand. Ship is going away. We must enter your city."

"Sir, I am... I am the prin– uh... She is – look, can we step inside the room for a moment? I..." He laid a palm gently on Kaiden's shoulder and pushed slightly, but it was like he had placed his hand on a solid rock face. Kaiden grimaced at the touch and gracefully slipped Cosmo's arm aside, moving past him to walk towards the captain.

Cosmo rushed to keep up. "Sir – sir! Ah– Sir! I–"

"Ship captain!" Kaiden exclaimed, striding up towards the Impalan. "You are to leave? We must get off. Now."

"Sir," Cosmo continued, breathless. "Let me explain, you see – we, we need to stay. Stay on the ship. I can't say why right now." His eyes flicked back and forth between the captain and Kaiden.

The captain sighed and looked directly into Kaiden's face, then barked simple short sentences. "King say no. No get off. You stay on ship."

Kaiden's face dissolved into a distorted mess of confusion. His ears drooped along with his shoulders, then he looked off at the city for a moment, before turning to Cosmo. "Why?! What offense I make?!"

"No! No offense!" Cosmo brought the palms of his hands up as if to defend himself, but he was careful not to touch Kaiden's broad chest. "Not your offense! Our! Our offense! Sir, please I–"

He was cut off by a rumble from the ship's engines. The deck vibrated strongly, then the vessel rose slowly upwards. Kaiden angrily blew out his breath, his face strained in embarrassed failure. He turned and stalked back towards the ship's guest quarters, slamming the door behind him. Cosmo winced his eyes shut and grimaced at the sound.

"I love me the politics," the captain grinned.

As the ship floated gently up and turned away from the glittering lights of the city, a dark figure that clung precariously to a dangling rope hoisted himself up hand over hand towards the stern.

eight

When she hunted to provide meat for the village, Jalendra knew respect for the animals they slaughtered. A sense of thankfulness at their sacrifice, and pride in her purpose when she returned with her kills.

All she felt now was guilt and shame.

In a daze she had walked aimlessly for over an hour, considering her kill while checking and re–checking the muscles of her arm and shoulder. They were not sore, exactly, or stretched or strained. They just seem to resonate with a chilling cold – a memory of the energy that had passed through them. She went over it again and again, letting the nausea come and go - to work through it. To somehow become used to it. She was certain of the color of the flames she'd seen, could imagine them in her mind and their detail. She didn't even have to strain to remember the conduit the feeling had taken through her body from her core out into the skrit.

As the dawn light began to fill the sky, she finally became aware of her exhaustion. Her eyes hurt – she was sure they were rimmed with red. She felt the chill on her arms and chest, the dew on her back, and the edges of hunger pains turning in her stomach. She sighed and turned in the direction of the village, trying to imagine how her master would explain her experience.

She knew she had somehow failed – something she'd never done before in her training. Why else would she feel this way? The knowledge twisted in her, wrapped around and through the tendrils of both the desire to again handle the fiery power, and the revulsion of the shame that seemed to overwhelm her when she used it.

She dropped instantly into a crouch.

All it had taken was the faintest twinge of the smell and her mind had barked its alarm. Her nostrils flared to catch more air. Desperately she worked her nose to gather and test what she'd just had the barest hint of. She tried and tried, but the air was clear. *So close? Did I come in upwind?*

She had – it was instinctive now for her to pick the right direction of approach to any location so prey could not smell her. She'd only gotten the edge of the rancid aroma when she'd been standing. Her head moved back and forth, eyes keenly scanning the brush around her. She saw nothing and smelled nothing. Frustrated, she slowly started to stand again, muscles tensed and heart beating faster.

She took a deep breath, and again caught the faintest twinge of a signature smell. Her eyes widened and she drew in deeply, catching a full waft of the stench.

Dirt and blood. Dark, thick soil twisted with the humus of rotting foliage and excrement, overlaid with a dank syrupy tang of dried blood. She blew breath out her nose to clear it and crouched down, her tail thumping to the ground from the speed of her motion.

Kem would be very upset with her if she had approached close enough to a Gorig to smell it but had not noticed the tell–tale signs of the creature's presence on the brush and the small animals nearby. She chided herself silently as she felt the pounding of her heart in her chest, and her two primary talons instinctively extended themselves. She could feel the anxiety drain from her shoulders – a Gorig was not small and helpless like a skrit. There should be no shame in this challenge. A Gorig would kill her for its own pleasure.

She tried to listen and to smell the air. But nothing came – as she crouched there was no scent at all. Curious. *I wonder if it's the same – can it smell me?*

It didn't matter. She felt a trained need to attack – to make a move. Kem would already have done so, she imagined. Unless the odds were known to be stacked against him, he would have barged forth into the thick of a fight. "Always attack. Do not hesitate," he had said to her. "Withdraw once you see how your first attack has fared. But the first attack must be to kill. Not to hurt. Not to test. Not to frighten. To kill – always to kill."

Jalendra stood, knees bent as she stepped away from the trees and started to walk slowly but purposefully out into the brush. She changed course only slightly once she got another waft of the smell of the creature, realizing it must be sleeping in a nearby depression in the ground. It would be able to hear her clearly now. Her heart thumped vibrations up into her throat, as she'd never gone after a Gorig alone. But she headed directly for it, eyes wide and ears standing straight up.

She heard the snap of a branch on the ground a few feet in front of her and it was enough – she launched herself forwards with a high–pitched Felid scream, taloned fists reared back to strike.

Seven feet tall and over three hundred pounds, the pitch black razor–toothed Gorig angrily leapt up to defend itself. The depression it had been sitting in was deep, and it had not had enough time after smelling and hearing Jalendra's approach to move to a spot that would make it less vulnerable.

Kem had been right – she had not hesitated and the advantage was hers. She came down upon the creature with her feet, gravity giving her thrusting legs more power as she kicked a pile–driver blow into its midsection. As she landed her arms thrust straight forward – impaling both her talons deep into its chest. It screamed and brought up its arms but by the time the creature's flailing claws had found her, their strength was already corrupted by the shock and damage of Jalendra's sudden attack. Shallow wounds were cut into her upper arms and shoulders but she felt no tearing of muscle.

On top of her prey as it fell backwards, she sprang using her bent knees and somersaulted over the shrieking beast, her talons tearing their way out of its chest. She landed and instantly turned with an almost 180–degree twist of her waist to mount a roundhouse kick. Her leg sliced through the air and the hard base of her heel caught the Gorig perfectly in its temple as it was scrambling to stand. With the crack of the impact it lurched sideways, staggered and then collapsed into a limp heap on the ground.

Jalendra gulped breath, standing perfectly still with all her senses screaming even the smallest bits of information at her. She filtered through it as sudden silence gripped the area – not even the barest hint of an animal or bird stirred the battle ground.

Is that it? she wondered. She glanced down at the thin cuts on her upper arms. *That's all I got from – from this?* She was surprised at herself, but nodded, proud for a moment as she stood up. *Now I kill it. Simple.*

She took two quick steps and withdrew her bloody talons to their sheathes, then used her fingers to touch down on the slimy wet fur around the creature's neck just below its chin. The stench was overwhelming, and she sipped short breaths. Blinking her eyes she tried to reach down into the hammering pulse of her heart, hoping the adrenaline of battle would help her access the same yellow fire she had touched with the skrit.

It did – almost immediately it was as if she somehow opened a door to a sealed room. She saw the yellow flames in her mind, and still caught in the rage of combat she felt the desperate desire to hold them, channel them. She would – knowing now what they would do and what they gave to her, in the moment she would relish in the glorious feeling of controlling that power. No matter what came after. Her mind grabbed it in fierce confidence.

But as she began to connect she felt something else.

Something beyond it – a flicker of deeper heat underneath it. A heat that was much stronger than the yellow flames. Different. Deep Red. Dark simmering red instead of yellow. Curious, she reached in her mind past the yellow licking flames, and instantly her chest felt full and her head light. An electric blast of shocking fear took her as heat billowed upwards.

She would be burned.

She should not touch it.

She would be burned.

Her throat constricted as it took everything in her conscious mind to quell the root animal instinct to pull away. The want to withdraw to the yellow flames that were her power. The yellow fulfilled everything she would ever need, ever want. Except... already she knew they were weaker. Weak as a candle to the sun.

In the screaming hurricane of the rush in her mind, all that was left – all that mattered – was her spirit. Her spirit, desperate to understand and know what was there at her center.

Kem didn't matter anymore. Nothing else mattered anymore.

She came over the top, rushing down to overwhelm her fear, the way that Kem always rushed her when they sparred. He was unstoppable then and she was unstoppable now – she grasped the fiery power and held it.

Her throat gargled a shuddered scream and her mouth dropped wide open in heart–stopping shock.

It hurt.

It hurt more than she felt she could bear. With a gaping mouth she gasped for a breath, arm shaking as she held her fingers on the exposed neck of the defeated beast in front of her. Her eyes saw her own shaking hand as she held and endured the gush of power from inside of her, felt the intense pain as she waited for it to do its job. The creature slit open its eyes, their faint light blearily staring back at her through a haze as it lay helpless in her death grip.

It was as if she lost her balance. As if she fell over one side of a precipice and tried desperately to catch onto something. Something that would save her – anything that could save her.

She did. She twisted the red blazing fire in her heart around, her mind willing up not threads of death but of life – connecting her spirit with the spirit of the dying Gorig in front of her. The harrowing flame she had fought to control overwhelmed her chest, her back, her arm, her hand. She moaned as it surged through her in a blasting radiance.

She let go, falling backwards to the ground.

The Gorig convulsed once and then suddenly rolled over, up and to standing. Its wide eyes took in Jalendra as she sat splayed on her rump, absolutely drained from the shock of the connection. The Gorig's paws moved to the spots where the Felid had pierced its chest with her talons, then to where she had landed on its gut. It made crude grunts as it felt its temple – not in pain but seemingly in confusion as it searched for its injuries.

There were none. All the damage Jalendra had inflicted was simply gone.

The Gorig shook its head in confusion and growled at her, but then took a quick step back, afraid. Another moment and it leapt away, bounding off into the brush.

Jalendra just sat in the dark, gulping breath with her head reeling as she listened to it run away. She felt a pain in her chest – in the same two places that she had skewered the Gorig with her talons. The heat was still there – the warmth of it throbbing. Holding her hand up to her breast she pressed and rubbed, moaning. It felt as if a narrow hole had been drilled right through her body. An empty hole ringed with burning embers.

nine

The sun had come up over the horizon minutes after the ship departed the city – Zefphyr's relatively short night and day cycles being something that inhabitants the world over both praised and cursed daily, depending on their individual needs. Cosmo stared upwards at the smear of orange and red the clouds made from the soft fire of the sun in the sky. He was almost never awake when the sun came up, and so was surprised at how it calmed him. Several layers of thick and thin ropes lay along the deck in front of the side wall and he thought of standing on them to look over the side, but he was still nervous after his near miss of getting squished by one of the large ones.

This was it, he thought. *This was supposed to be my last day responsible for her.* He sighed. *Now I've got another seven or eight days of it, at least.*

"It's beautiful," Saira spoke as she leaned next to him at the rail. "I love the sunrise – my... visitors... the ones you don't manage to scare away. I've watched it with them from the tower when we've had a late night," she grinned.

"Yes, well." Cosmo sighed and did not look at her, continuing to stare off at the light. "Not a normal thing for me. I sleep, I eat, and I watch over you. Not sunrises."

"How did it go? Where is the ambassador?"

"I did my best, so of course it went terribly," Cosmo stated flatly. "He thinks he offended us and that we're sending him home."

"Oh, Cosmo," she said lightly, touching his arm to reassure him. "Don't worry about it. Where is he now?"

"In the guest cabin over there. He went back into it as we were leaving. I had to come over here to take a moment, then I was going to get you. So you could fix things."

"Hm. All right. Well, now that we've left I can move around freely and go see him, tell him what's going on." She departed the rail and started to walk across the deck.

"Oh, and... he's uh... he's cute," Cosmo added, breaking his stare from the clouds as they started to lose the morning color. He looked sideways at her as she stopped walking and turned to him with a curious and playful smile.

"He's an ambassador, princess," Cosmo warned.

"So... he's definitely not stupid, then."

Oh crap.

Cosmo turned back to look again up and off the side of the ship, bringing his hand up to his forehead then running it slowly past his glasses and down his face. He heard the guest door open and close as she went inside, but staunchly refused to follow her. *I've done enough damage for this morning.*

It took him another half hour to work up the courage but eventually he moved to stand on top of the layers of ropes, gingerly placing his feet on them to approach the boat's side rail. From there, he distracted himself by watching the rocks and dirty brown desert to the south of the city pass by a couple of hundred feet underneath, before it gave way to the black char of the dead zone.

He'd never seen it before – only heard about it. Cinders and ash, scorched sharp rocks and shattered hills, but not one solitary living thing. Not now nor for the past thousand cycles, since the Meltdown. For miles and miles and miles. He expected to see blown tendril clouds of black dust, but even the wind seemed to avoid the huge expanse of death. Cosmo knew that hundreds of cycles ago, condemned criminals were even exiled to the wasteland to die of hunger and thirst. Still, people had explored it. Some had even been obsessed with it – certain it held hidden treasures left by the Masters before their destruction. But most simply avoided it, as they would avoid a huge expanse of open water. Nothing of interest, nothing of value.

Quickly bored by the black devastation, Cosmo retired to their small hold in the forecastle. He found his case and cleaned his spectacles, and tried not to think about what would happen to them if the ship lost power and crashed into the huge expanse of ash. He relaxed against a soft pile of textiles bound into a roll, and decided to close his eyes for a moment.

He awoke two hours later to the smell of salty broth, and instinctively licked his lips. Removing his glasses he rubbed his eyes and blinked, slowly remembering why he was in a small cramped space. Opening the door to his compartment a sliver, he spied Miss Stan and another deckhand placing bread and a steaming bowl of soup onto the large wooden table that took up half the deck space under the main mast. His hunger pushed him up onto his feet, but his fatigue betrayed his memory and his head smacked into the roof of the compartment again.

He winced, moaning, then opened the door fully and emerged out onto the deck. Looking around, besides those setting the table he spied the captain up on the aft deck manning the ship's controls. There was no sign of the princess or the ambassador. He looked worriedly at the door to the guest quarters.

As if on cue, the door opened and a laugh from the princess burst through, followed by a hearty deeper chuckling from the ambassador. Saira held her stomach with one hand as she giggled and came out onto the deck, turning to reach her other hand back and beckon Kaiden to come out with her.

Cosmo swallowed and sighed. *How long was I asleep?* In the palace there was a morning meal and an evening meal, and on special occasions a single meal mid–day. *Did I miss the morning meal, or is this the only one they have in a day?* he wondered. He shuffled towards the main table on the deck but kept his eyes on the princess as she continued listening to whatever hilarious story the ambassador was telling her.

"No, I have learned well from the ships that come," Kaiden said to her, finishing a thought. "I take trips with them. I work. And talk. I learn to swear like a sailor – you would like that I teach you?"

She laughed again, then looked around to let her eyes find Cosmo. "Well," she answered Kaiden. "At least not while Cosmo or my father are around."

"It is agreed," Kaiden smiled and followed her gaze to Cosmo. His speech was stilted but it was already becoming smoother, as if he was learning very fast the subtleties of northern speech patterns. Cosmo was even more worried he was definitely not stupid.

"I apologize!" Kaiden exclaimed loudly, coming away from Saira and taking steps towards Cosmo. Her attendant smiled weakly, and extended his hand to shake in greeting. Kaiden gripped his hand and pulled it to his chest near where Cosmo had touched him before, but treated the extremity as if it was a cherished treasure. "Please do not be angry, Mister Cosmo! Princess Saira has explain to me. She has told me of your bravery and of your love. You are her protector and I wish to be a friend."

Cosmo gulped, and his eyes widened but he smiled, lightly squeezing the hands that seemed to covet his. "Well, Ambassador Kaiden, I am your servant as I am hers."

Kaiden smiled again – a wide grin that lit up his whole face with deep honesty. "You make me happy! Come – let us sit and eat food."

They all took places at the table, Saira across from Cosmo and Kaiden at her side. She even patted the bench close beside her before he sat down. When he did, she grinned before turning to her food. Cosmo swallowed hard and sighed. *Oh boy. She's got it bad already.* Cosmo bit into the bread and then sipped some broth, but his mind was already lost in how to talk to the princess about using restraint with the young male.

"Sounds like you two were having quite the conversation," Cosmo said suggestively.

"We were speaking of ships that come to my people," Kaiden said as he took some broth for himself. "And about the Masters... the Masters a long time ago. I go – uh, went – on the ships. The sailors – they teach me to speak your... words, and they tell me many things they have seen and know," Kaiden explained. "The Masters were Humans, but not like today. They were not of planet."

"Well, yes. Everyone knows that," Cosmo stated flatly.

Saira tilted her head forward and frowned at him to show her disapproval at his tone.

"Yes, but they could not even breathe here!" Kaiden continued, touching his hand to his mouth and nose for emphasis. "Their bodies were all wrong. Their blood, even their... hide? ...skin. It was wrong. Not right for the... bugs. And too thin for our wind and rain. Outside, like this..." he said as he gestured around them. "Too cold. They would be sick very soon. They would die."

"So they changed themselves," Saira nodded. "And at the same time made us... from you. Your kind."

"And from other types, yes." Kaiden smiled, obviously pleased with himself that he was able to carry a conversation in a language he was still getting used to. "But inside their machines – doing the mating with blood and with... all other parts of bodies, and with the energy of planet." He used his hands to emphasize small and big.

Cosmo listened to them as Kaiden openly explained the differences between the bodies of the northern, genetically engineered felids and the unaltered aboriginals. He was completely immodest in his description of even private body parts, and the princess hung on his every word – fascinated at his honesty and an apparent lack of fear of saying something inappropriate.

"I understand why the Masters changed some things in us from you," Saira said to Kaiden. "But it's some of the cosmetic things that I always wonder about. The tail is the most interesting to me – I think that would be fantastic!" she exclaimed. She laughed and put her hands on her hips in mock indignation. "Why can't I have a tail?! Why did they take it off for us? It's so silly."

"Oh, I hate my tail many times," Kaiden grinned, but brought his up behind his back in between them. He easily laid its thickness across his hand and then bluntly held it out to her.

Saira's eyes widened and she brought a hand to her mouth in surprise. Cosmo coughed as he choked on a bit of bread in his mouth.

Kaiden's eyes dropped and he looked surprised, suddenly aware that he may have done something inappropriate. But it was abundantly clear the end of his tail was not an especially private part of his body. Saira blinked, swallowed, then summoned her bravery and very carefully reached out to touch the end of it. It flicked upwards in her hand once and she giggled.

Kaiden persevered, as she did. "It has thinking.. without my thinking. It can ruin... talking – people talking. My female friend, Jalendra. She is very good with her tail – it does not get in her way."

"You have a female friend?" Cosmo injected with a quick smile and a demure glance at Saira. "A wife?"

Saira shot back an ice cold look of her own, but then jerked her head around to anxiously wait for Kaiden's answer.

"No. My father's... student. She cannot be... as wife... while she is a student."

"Oh, but... maybe when she's finished?" Cosmo nodded in encouragement, offering the natural possibility.

Kaiden looked slightly confused at Cosmo's tone for a moment, and looked back and forth between Saira and her attendant. Kaiden swallowed the bread in his mouth and for the second time in moments he looked as though he was worried he had said something wrong. "I... am surprised. The females are required to... be as wife?"

"No!" Saira expressed, irritated as she waved Cosmo quiet. "We decide who we are with, when and for how long. We don't let the males tell us what to do." She turned to look simply at Cosmo. "Or not to do."

Kaiden brightened. "Ah, well, it is... uh... com–pat–i–ble... with us. I am sorry, Mister Cosmo. I do not wish to make assumptions and Princess Saira has made me, perhaps, excited and eager to... talk. Learn more about your people."

"Oh, I'm excited and eager to learn more, too," Saira countered, softly, placing her elbows on the table and her chin on her closed hands as she gazed at the handsome ambassador.

Oh crap. Crap! Crap! Crap!

"Jalendra – she is your father's student," Cosmo stated, trying to stay on a topic that might slow down the princess. "What does she – or she and your father – do, Ambassador Kaiden?"

"My father is, in our language, *Pilla*. There are always three, in any village of my people I have visited."

"*Pilla*", Saira echoed, liking the taste of her first foreign word. "The leaders?"

"Yes, they – guide us. In diff–"

"So you're the leader's son," Cosmo interjected again, surprised. "You are a prince?"

"No! Oh – I am sorry Mister Cosmo. That is wrong." He rolled his eyes for a moment, smiling. "My father would be very upset to hear that."

"I'm sorry, ambassador," Cosmo looked worried, and Saira cocked her brows, not understanding the sudden disconnect.

"No, no, heheh. Please do not be upset," Kaiden chuckled. "It is natural for you to think this. There are three *Pilla* – one is healer, feeding the... calm? of the people, mind and body. Is 'calm' the right word?"

"Yes, I think we understand," Saira confirmed. "They're healers – doctors or psychologists–"

"Psy–col... Psycolgie..." Kaiden started, questioning the word.

"Never mind, I'm sorry. That is a difficult word. Healers is probably better."

"Yes, healers," Kaiden continued. "They remove things that stop... get in the way of... uh... love."

"Love?" Saira queried, cocking a brow. Cosmo was unsettled at where the conversation might go, especially after Kaiden's blunt descriptions of bodies. But also could not help his curiosity.

"Yes, love," Kaiden said with a smile, deciding that the word was appropriate. "All love. Love of sky, love of ground," he motioned with his hands. "Love in taste of food, of warmth when it is cold."

"Ah," Cosmo stated. "I thought you meant love for people."

"Love of people it can be also, like you Cosmo," Kaiden added.

"Like me?" Cosmo was confused.

"Yes, Princess Saira has told me of your love for her."

"Oh no!", Cosmo looked taken aback. "No – I mean.. wait. That's a kind of love, but uh..." He couldn't fathom how to describe the distinction between romantic love and other types of love without embarrassing himself.

"Kaiden, what is your word for this love?" Saira interjected.

"*Viada*", Kaiden said easily.

The princess smiled and looked into the aboriginal's amber eyes. "And is there a different word for love between two people who are... together as one? Mated? Say, if... Cosmo had a wife?"

Cosmo rolled his eyes at the suggestion.

"Ah, yes," Kaiden said easily. "*Vasha*".

"*Vasha*" Saira repeated, without breaking her gaze at him. "That word has a nice sound."

Cosmo cleared his throat, the exaggeration of which caused Saira to turn to look at him. He gave her a disapproving glare. "Your father is a healer?" Cosmo queried to Kaiden without breaking his gaze at the princess.

"No, no." Kaiden had to chuckle again as he looked skyward with raised brows – a gesture apparently universal enough that he had already caught onto it. "My father is warrior *Pilla*. They fight, hunt. Protect the village and people. Provide meat."

"I see," Cosmo nodded, glancing at the princess. "So he's like, big and strong and mean–"

"Cosmo!" Saira exclaimed.

"Hah – yes, mean!" Kaiden exclaimed. "Rarrrgh!" he made an angry face and put up reared hands, clawing the air.

Saira burst out laughing, putting a hand to her mouth to stifle the sound as she shook. Cosmo had to laugh at the sound the princess made, finding it hard to contain his own amusement at the image Kaiden provided.

Saira caught her breath. "Well, we'll be very careful when we meet him. What about the third *Pilla* – you said there were three?"

"Yes, the third is what we call *Ormah Tee Chu Tah*," Kaiden explained, using more words in his aboriginal tongue. "They bring other... needed... things. Food – not meat, but other food. They make shelter, clothing."

"So, healers, warriors, and *Ormah Tee Chu Tah*," Saira summarized, roughly approximating the right words in the foreign language. "Uh.. 'providers'?"

"Seems like it," Cosmo nodded. "Pretty simple."

"Yes, simple," Kaiden agreed. "In the village you choose a path – healer, warrior, or... pro–vi–der. You follow the *Pilla* for the path. If something happens to the village, the *Pilla* must decide together, then the people do what is decided."

"Hm," Saira pondered aloud. "So... things like my visit. The *Pilla* decided that you could come to the Empire – and that you could take me back with you?"

"Yes, two of three must agree. That was what happened."

"Let me guess," Cosmo said slyly. "Your father...?"

"My father did not agree or disagree. He did not care. The others both agreed, so I am here, as are you."

"But what... path... are you on, Kaiden?" Saira asked, cocking her head to the side. "You're don't seem to be a warrior. Are you a healer, or a provider?"

Kaiden appeared uncomfortable for a moment, and looked downward. Cosmo felt briefly pleased that he was not the only one capable of saying something inappropriate.

"I... I was a warrior, once. Like my father." He swallowed and then looked up into Saira's eyes. "But I– my mother and I– felt... I could not follow that path. So I have found my own. I choose myself what I do, where I go."

Saira smiled brightly, breathing a soft sigh as she looked into his face.

"Ah, but I am forgetting myself!" Kaiden suddenly stood, knocking against the table as he extracted himself from the bench. "I must have captain send a signal to my village. I must tell them we are arriving today at night. They are expect us to arrive in five days!"

"Oh dear," Saira exclaimed. "I'd forgotten you needed to do that!" She turned and looked up at Captain Fasil, who was still at the wheel controlling the airship. "He can help you, I think."

"Yes, I go. I will return," he bowed and stepped away towards the short staircase that led up to the aft deck.

Cosmo didn't say a thing to the princess, and didn't look at her. He got up from the table and walked away slowly towards the side of the ship. With no hesitation he stepped up onto the ropes and gripped the rail, staring off into the clouds. It took a minute, but she followed him and tugged on his robe to make him turn to face her.

"He's very nice, Cosmo," she said softly. "Why are you so upset?"

"Because he's very nice," Cosmo bit out, exasperated. "And he's an ambassador. And he's the son of one of their leaders. And I can see, plain as day that you're already thinking of him in ways you shouldn't."

"Well..." she smiled. "It's hard not to like him, and I've got an imagination, sure. If I keep it in my head, I can... amuse myself. He's.. how did you put it? Gentle and kind, strong but thoughtful."

And bonus if he's good looking. Cosmo shut his eyes and wished he could have told his past self to shut up. "Well, you know that there are more things at stake here than your amusement, mental or physical. You're a visiting dignitary. Don't try to–"

"Oh Cosmo," she responded dismissively. "I can control myself."

"Mmmm... You do tend to rush in, my dear child."

She was silent for a moment, staring at him and forming her response in her head. "You know what? I'm not a child. I'm eighteen today. I get to choose where I go and what I do. Not you. Not my father. Me."

Cosmo rolled his eyes, chiding himself. *Don't bring logic to an emotional argument.* He huffed a breath. "Just... please don't get hurt. And please don't lead him along."

"I like him. If he's part of my future I'm certain it will be a pleasant part. I couldn't imagine hurting him," she said, turning to walk away in Kaiden's direction.

What you can't imagine is what I'm afraid of.

ten

Wrapped in his hooded cloak, Ogren peered through a crack in the bulkhead of the hold of the *Daedalus* and watched the crewmembers finish their meal in the galley. The Human had water in his hip flask, but no food of his own. He could smell the broth and the bread, and his stomach ached and growled. It was hours since they'd left Carnarvon and he hadn't been able to move from his hiding spot. He listened to the Impalan crew talking about the princess.

"Why they ain't on a Navy ship?" Miss Stan muttered in between mouthfuls of bread. "Navy ship's got guns. Fine people. Much safer than here. They don't trust their own?"

"Navy docks were empty when we were in, I saw," a rigger answered her. "We touched in no more than two marks and we're out again. They couldn't wait no longer'n that."

"Still don't make sense. Royals don't go runnin' about all secret like this."

"Musta been some hullybaloo," the cook said as he stirred the broth on the stove. "Maybe somebody wanna hurt that ambassador guy. Maybe somebody don't like him and he's important. So they send her to look after him, so's he don't get all mad."

"He's just a southern scruff," the rigger countered dismissively. "Hah, right. Ambassador. Pssh. Them kind from the bush don't care about stuff like that. Ain't seen or heard'a no ambassador from them before."

Excellent, Ogren thought with a smile. *An ambassador. Somebody to take the blame when I kill her. I needed that.* He knew that the princess hadn't come aboard alone – his spy near the docks had said her attendant was with her. Him and possibly Captain Valaria. The palace guard captain would certainly have been a problem – everyone who lived below the belt typically both revered and detested her. Luckily as Ogren had rushed to the docks he'd seen Valaria on the main street, moving away back towards the belt. That left only the slight attendant, the ambassador, and whatever crew were on board, between him and his goal.

Ogren had heard about the princess' journey to the docks from one of his tavern spotters. Rushing to respond to the information, he'd instinctively grabbed a two-shot spike gun and a cloak as he departed his lair. He'd been very careful with the long heavy pistol so far, but now was having second thoughts about its usefulness. The southern felids didn't use guns, and the Impalan crew wouldn't have theirs out of an arms locker without the captain's knowledge. So if he used it to kill the princess it would be simple to determine there had been an assassin. He couldn't leave it on the ship to be found afterwards – but without a solid plan he also couldn't bring himself to just toss it over the side. He looked down to the floor beside him where the gun lay and grimaced at it. *Baggage.*

Hard footsteps came from the stairs leading up to the main deck, and Captain Fasil poked his head down under the opening to observe his crew. They all stopped eating and looked at him expectantly.

"Forest's teeth are comin' up in a mark or so. We're past the ash and nothin' we could bump into for a while so we're on auto guide. Weather's clear and air's even so you can all sleep a bit. Be busy later when we get in, so take the time. I'm certainly gunna." He paused, then came down the last few steps to the lower deck and walked towards the galley table. "Gimme some bread, will you?"

Ogren grinned. *Perfect. Nobody on deck and crew mostly asleep. Simply wait a few minutes, then go up on deck.* Then he could improvise – or if the princess was alone for a moment he could quietly strangle her.

He shifted from his cramped seated position behind some barrels and peered from under the rim of his hood at the trap–hatch that led backwards toward the engine room. The Human rubbed his rope–burned hands and winced. Climbing up the side of the ship from the bottom to the engine vents while carrying a gun had been more physical work than he'd done in a long time. Doing it again on an empty stomach with no sleep was going to be even worse.

It's gonna be worth it, he reminded himself.

eleven

Cosmo had slept for another hour after the meal. The bread and warm broth from the meal in his belly and the complete lack of sleep the night before made it simple for him to snooze in the little compartment in the foredeck of the ship. When he woke he could tell the sunlight was starting to fade.

It's a day's trip so we must be getting close, he thought to himself. He yawned and cleaned his spectacles on his robe, then pushed them onto his face and wiggled his nose to let them settle. Standing up in the cramped space again, this time he put his hand up to touch the low ceiling and ease his head near it rather than smack into it. He smiled at his improving memory and opened the door, glancing out onto the deck.

Saira was at the rail nearby, standing on the ropes looking wistfully up into Kaiden's face as her hand wrapped around his back to rest on his muscular shoulders. She began to lean in closer to him as if to whisper something in his ear.

"Hey! I–" Cosmo surged forward and bonked his forehead on the frame of the portal. "Ow!" He stepped through and cursed very loudly.

"Hah! I know what that one means!" Kaiden exclaimed.

"Cosmo, are you all right?" Saira fretted. She came away from Kaiden and stepped down off the ropes to put a hand to Cosmo's forehead. "That sounded terrible."

"Yes," he muttered in annoyance. "Sorry – I will have to try to improve the sound of my head hitting things."

She hunched her brows and gave his tone a scolding look. "We were just talking about you. Kaiden wants to know all about your job as an attendant."

"Hmph!" He rubbed his head and waved away her hand. "Well, what did you tell him already?"

"I said you've looked after me since I was six. That I was upset that father gave me a male attendant, and one so young. I was certain I didn't need you." She smiled into his face. "I was so wrong."

"She says you are good, Mister Cosmo. She tells me of her happiness with you." Kaiden said brightly.

"Well, I'm pretty much finished now," he sighed. He didn't know why, but he turned away from the princess and deliberately avoided her gaze as he finished his statement. "Just ask her – she's eighteen today and doesn't care what I say any more."

He could imagine her reaction in his head – crossed arms over her chest and a hurt expression. It made his cheeks burn and he feigned interest in one of the thicker ropes, kicking at it to try to kick the vision out of his mind. Saira brusquely brushed past him and stepped up onto the pile, alighting next to Kaiden.

Cosmo sighed but joined them, moving to Kaiden's other side as they all took in the view off the side of the ship. The sun was beginning to set through the clouds. The dark scar of the dead zone had passed while Cosmo was asleep, and now they were over thick forests and bush that sharp rocks protruded through.

"We must be getting close," Cosmo murmured aloud.

"Yes, it is not far now," Kaiden said. He pointed down to indicate a wide expanse of jagged rocks the ship had been flying over. "These are the Teeth of the Forest," he explained. "They protect it from outside. They are difficult... mean. We do not go past them except if on ship. Many of my people will never travel past these rocks."

A hooded deckhand approached from behind them, shambling up to clear his throat. "Don't you mind me. I gotta start getting the boat ready for docking now. It's harder to do in the dark so I'm doing it now."

"Of course," Saira responded happily, turning as she intended to step down off the layers of ropes. "Are we in your way?"

"Naw, naw, s'ok." He put the palm of his hand up to signal her to stay. "Just... stand right where ya are. Don't ya move while I adjust the rope things." The man reached beside Cosmo and freed a line that strung its way up to the aft mast.

"There we go. One more on the other side." He moved around the three of them to get it.

"Rope things?" Cosmo inquired with an amused snigger. "Is that the technical term?"

Saira chuckled. "Cosmo, let him do his job."

"S'far as you know that's what they are," the Human grumbled and then turned to walk towards the capstan near the main mast.

"He's the first non–Impalan I've seen on this ship," Cosmo muttered. "I thought the whole crew was supposed to be Impalan. I prefer them – much more polite."

"Impalans – Heh!" Kaiden smiled, looking off into the fading light of the evening. "Now they know how to swear!"

A curse was more than appropriate as bundles of the ropes sprang up from between their feet, jamming against their knees and crotches to fling them powerfully upwards and over the side of the ship.

Cosmo heard Saira scream over his own yell of shocked surprise. His light body flew through the air and he caught a glimpse of the side of the ship pass by as he fell away from it towards the gray crags of razor–sharp rocks hundreds of feet below. But just in that instant he felt the twist of a thinner rope around his leg, starting to pull on the fabric of his robe. This was followed by a yank as it pulled taut, and he suddenly found himself swinging violently back and forth upside–down hanging under the hull of the ship. He continued to yell in terror, jerking his head around to try to figure out what had happened.

He saw Kaiden's robe – a flash of red as the aboriginal Felid was stretched out. One arm was up as he desperately hung onto a rope with one hand, and one arm was down as that hand clutched the back of the princess' cloak. Saira hung there and continued to scream and flail in terror, legs kicking as she reached her arms up to her neck to hold onto her cloak.

Cosmo looked up to see the rope caught around his leg, then past his feet at the side of the sky boat. The Human deckhand was there, and shoved his hood back and away in frustration. Below a half–shaved head of white hair, the man's face was scrunched up in angry disappointment, and in his hands Cosmo saw the flash of a knife blade.

Cosmo yelped and screamed, turning his bugged eyes wildly downwards to find Kaiden and Saira.

"He's going to cut it! Kaiden! He's going to–"

Kaiden let go of the rope.

Cosmo's yelling voice was suddenly quelled by a huge lump that shot up into his throat at the sight of the falling princess. Unable to pull his eyes away, he twisted to see them fall towards the rocks he knew would shred them.

His heart squeezed tight as he watched them during the long fall, until at the last moment he was surprised they hit the shallow water of a large clear lake that had just barely come underneath them. Kaiden had timed the fall, letting go at the perfect moment so they missed the rocks, and missed the deep water. The lump in Cosmo's throat vanished and a shiver went over his body. He started yelling again looked back up towards their nemesis on the ship. The half–bald man's face was red from anger and Cosmo could hear him cursing. *What is he doing?!* Cosmo's mind blazed in through irrelevant and competing questions. *Who is he?! Is he cutting my rope? What do I do?!* The fear screamed in his mind as he hung upside down. He looked at the rope that held his leg, then jerked his face to look downwards at the ground. The *Daedalus* was moving at its regular sluggish clip, but they would still reach the end of the wide lake in a moment. There was nothing but more sharp rocks after that.

He looked up and saw the flash of the blade of the knife against the rope holding him up – but it wasn't moving, wasn't sawing – not yet. Their attacker was waiting until he cleared the short lake, waiting so that he could watch Cosmo fall and smash onto the rocks.

Desperately he pulled himself up and fumbled with the rope that had tangled around his leg and ankle. He did not take a breath first and his compressed stomach made him gasp and try to suck in air that would not come as his thin fingers clawed at the stuck extremity. His stomach muscle gave out and he fell back down to hang straight upside down again, sucking in air in a heaving screech of noise.

The strong yanking motion of his backward fall freed his leg, and he became instantly untangled. He fell – over and over, head over heels, until the back of his head smacked into the water of the ice cold lake.

twelve

Jalendra returned to the village well into the afternoon – completely unsure of what she was going to tell Kem about what had happened. There was blood on her primary talons and on her hands, and the fresh cuts on her shoulders and upper arms stood out. But she didn't have a carcass to show for her time in the wilderness.

But I held the power, she thought. *I controlled it. That was what I was supposed to do.*

But it hadn't killed the way it was supposed to. In fact, it seemed to have the opposite effect. The Gorig should have died from its injuries alone – she was sure she'd punctured one of its lungs and ripped through vital parts of its circulatory system. There was no way it could have gotten up and run away like it did. Unless its wounds had somehow been reversed. She'd channeled her power into it – pushed through the yellow flames and gone beyond them to the deep red. Had she given the creature some piece of it? A piece of her life?

Thick walls of ironwood ran the perimeter of the village, shielding it from the natural ravages of the forest. Whenever Jalendra returned from an outing, she usually looked to their tops, to see which sentries were present and to wave and smile to them. This time her brows were hunched down and she focused entirely on the gate. She could hear the call of a young male to open the gate for her, but she could barely raise her tired eyes from the ground.

The youngest children had tired themselves out for the day, and so a serene quiet was all that greeted her. Methodical plodding led her away from the wall toward the cooking fires. The boars that had been collected and cooked in the morning were down to their bones – tough sinews of meat that were the only parts left. She could feel the twisted grimace on her face as she crouched by the fire and gnawed at what she could for sustenance.

"You return," Kem said as he approached from behind her, an air of inquisition in his voice.

She remained still except for her fingers manipulating the bones to get at the small strings of meat she was able to salvage. She was normally relaxed in his presence; usually eager to talk about what she had learned during a hard lesson. But for some reason this time she felt no desire to connect with him. *You didn't tell me,* she thought. *You didn't prepare me properly.* She stopped biting at the bone in her hand and threw it into the fire, closing her eyes to think for a moment.

He kneeled, dropping soundlessly next to her, the crimson of his dark red robe visible at her periphery. He said nothing more and she ignored him while concentrating on how to explain what she felt.

"I used my power," she said at last.

"Where is your kill?" Kem asked, confused.

"I killed a skrit rat. And defeated a Gorig."

"A Gorig?" Kem brightened. He sniffed with his nose past the smell of the fire and the charred meat, and smiled when the scent still faintly on her was brought to his senses. "A baby or..."

"Full size. A male. I received these.." she ran her palms over the cuts on her arms, but did not look at him. "But nothing more."

He blinked in surprise, opened his mouth, then closed it. She'd never experienced him speechless before.

"You have been trained well, Jalendra. You honor me and our clan with your skill," he said, almost chuckling. "I am proud to be your teacher."

"I used my power – I found it. Held it. After the skrit it was easy to find it. The yellow flames... burned me. As you said they would. I endured."

Kem exhaled a loud breath of relief, as if he had expected her words and was proud of himself at his own prediction.

"But I did not kill the Gorig."

She was not turned to him, but she could still feel Kem's relief wash away like a receding wave on a beach. She imagined his brows hunched down in confusion. "I do not understand."

She licked her lips and swallowed, still not turning to face him. Her eyes devoured the remaining embers of the cooking fire. He knew she was telling the truth. There was no way she could lie to him, or him to her – the cycles of training had proven that to both of them. All they ever spoke to each other was the truth. All they ever had to force themselves to ask of each other was what they needed to know.

"I barely touched the skrit. The flames – I felt the yellow. They were simple," she shuddered as she recalled the feeling. "It came up – out of me. Through my arm." Her voice was listless, as if she was describing a dream. "It hurt, but it was easy...." *Easy compared to what came after.*

"Yes, yes, that is the power," he blurted. "Exactly. If you felt that you held it."

"But with the Gorig...", her eyes widened as she remembered and her voice quieted. "I found the red."

Kem was silent.

"You never told me of the red," she whispered, shaking her head slightly.

"I do not understand," Kem stated flatly. "I do not understand red. There is no red. You–"

"It was so much more," she continued wistfully, cutting him off. "Up through my back, my arms, my face, my chest. I felt it. The burning and the light. Red fire. And not for a short time. It – it felt like forever."

Jalendra could hear Kem's confused breathing turn to frustration as he sought to fathom what she had experienced. But she was not trying to please him. Or to teach him. She was explaining to herself as must as she was to him.

"I held its throat," she stated firmly. "I went past your yellow. I pulled my power – my red power – through myself into it." She turned to face him, wide eyes looking into his face.

"And? What happened? What happened to the Gorig?" he demanded.

She looked into his eyes as she had looked into the Gorig's eyes. Trying to make him understand.

"I looked at it. At its eyes, and... inside of it. And it looked back at me. Inside of me."

Kem sat in silence and stared at her, the lines on his face drawing harder, trying to conceive of what had happened to Jalendra. "It... looked... at you? And?"

"It was afraid – it was hurt. It had given up."

"You defeated it! It knew its death was coming!" There was anger in his voice now – incredulous anger and confusion at the nonsense she was spouting at him. "You have seen this before! Why did you stop?!"

"I did not stop!" she retorted. Kem's eyes widened at her outburst, but she pushed past his silent rebuke. She needed to say it and he needed to shut up and listen.

"I used my power – all of it! I let it loose, through me. But it changed from what I thought it was. My mind... connected. I saw the Gorig's eyes and my mind connected with it. I felt its fear and its loss and its coming death. That was all there was. And then..."

"It's not possible!" Kem seethed, shaking his head.

"It happened!" she yelled at him, her voice cracking in fear. "My... my red fire – not your yellow. It came out, it took over. I did not think it could be controlled – there was no way I could stop it. But it did what I wanted it to do." Her voice quieted as her mind seized on the words and their truth. "It did what I wanted," she repeated.

Kem was silent, his glistening eyes showing a blazing fire of confusion. His shoulders were high and tight to his body, and his arms gripped his chest as if he was going to rip himself apart. "It did what you wanted," he echoed, his voice shaking.

Jalendra nodded. "The Gorig got up," she said, even more quietly. "It got up – as if I had not even touched it. Its wounds – gone. Healed. Completely, as if they were never there. It was dying... and then it was healed. It just got up and it ran away."

Kem closed his eyes and turned his head down towards the ground. His face began to contort, and he quickly brought his hands up to his face, covering it to hide an overwhelming shame from her eyes.

Jalendra was absolutely shocked – she'd never seen Kem make such a gesture, or act in such a manner. Never. It was as if he had instantly become someone else – like a shell had shattered and fallen from his body.

"Master! What is... What does this mean?" She slowly reached out her hand to him.

Without a word Kem turned and started to walk slowly towards the huts of the village. His arms came down to clutch across his chest and hold himself tightly as he shuffled away.

Jalendra stood alone at the fireside, staring in complete loss at his back.

thirteen

Cosmo could see her clearly. It was the first time in cycles he'd been able to do so. She sat next to the bed, leaning over a small shivering form wrapped in blankets. She hummed softly, in rhythms he could feel were imprinted in his past. It was going to be all right. He would get better. He was through the worst of it. He just needed to sleep.

"Mother," he said to her. He stepped closer to the bed and looked down – down at himself. Only a child, sick. Still fighting the pneumonia that had almost claimed him.

She looked up at him, smiling easily, knowing that he was there and happy to see him. A ripple of confusion moved across her face, but washed away as quickly as it had come. "You'll get better," she murmured as she looked back down on his younger self. "You got better," she sighed happily as she closed her eyes.

"I do. I am."

"Are you dreaming?" she said, as if to the child in the bed.

He felt the tautness of the muscles in his face as he smiled. "Of course I'm dreaming."

She opened her eyes and looked up at him, and the confusion was back across her face, lingering longer this time before it gradually drained away. His breath seemed to catch in his throat as he saw her unsettled visage.

"This is... different," he said tentatively.

"Yes. How?"

"I can see you now. Your face. I haven't been able to. For cycles now." His voice cracked and he settled on his knees on the far side of the bed from her. He could feel himself straining against tears of guilt.

"Oh, Cosmo, it's all right. I can always see you, whenever I want to. Clear as I can right now. Like you're right...", she said as her face turned to the child form in the bed. "Like you're right here."

"I am here," he said, almost a squeak as he tried desperately to hold back the gush of a cry. "I'm not going to leave."

"But you have to," she said softly, reaching forward to tuck the blankets up around the child. "How else are you going to grow up?"

"I am grown up. I have – I have my life."

The frail form in the bed had stopped shivering, and while swaddled tightly in the blankets he started to breathe more deeply and easily as he slept. Cosmo watched his mother stroke the flop of hair on the child's head away from his face and hold her palm against his cheek for a moment.

"I'm not going to leave," he repeated more strongly.

She drew her hand back from the child, and turned to put her index finger in front of her lips, shushing him. Cosmo swallowed and turned his eyes down to the bed covers before responding softly. "I'm not."

"Leaving you was hard," she said. "You needed me. You were big – seventeen, if I remember correctly. But..."

He looked up at her and she was smiling, her soft eyes holding him the same way that they had held the child form of himself that lay in the bed.

"But you needed me," she continued, finding her words. "You had... changes. Some growing left to do. I wasn't there to guide you the way I should have been."

"I want to see you like this," he said with an edge of desperation in his voice. "I want to be with you like this."

"You are. I have you here with me."

"It's not like this for me – normally."

She smiled, and her voice turned into a playful question. "What would it be like, to have me back again. In your life, for real? Not in a dream."

"It would make my life complete," he said, his voice turning into a pleading as the idea came out of the shroud of impossibility as she spoke the words.

"It would give you a foundation?"

"Yes."

"It would give you love? Friendship?"

"Yes, the best kind. The kind I want. That I need."

"But would it push you to grow and change?"

He was silent for a moment. Her eyes watched him, her mouth still a smile as her head slowly tilted to one side, coaxing a response from him.

"I don't want to grow and change."

His mother smiled sadly, eyes suddenly wet and cheeks tight as she swallowed. She glanced at the child in the bed. "Oh, Cosmo."

Cosmo felt his cheeks burn from the childishness of his own comment.

"Are you the foundation for someone? Do you have a child?"

"No, not my own. But she is– "

"Do you give love?"

"Yes."

"Do you give friendship? The best kind?"

Cosmo huffed a breath out his nose and stared into his mother's eyes. He had no need to speak – she knew everything in him. Loved everything in him.

"You have growing and changing left to do. And not just for yourself. If I could, I would have stayed with you, when you needed me. Wouldn't that have been best?"

He closed his eyes and felt the familiarity of her in the words. The soft and strong instinctual foundation she'd built that he relied on and trusted. The very base of who he was. She was there. Even in the blackness with his eyes closed.

"I love you Cosmo..."

He saw her mouth move, and she said something else, but he couldn't hear it. A warble of her voice disappearing into a sloshing sound of water. He tried to open his eyes but couldn't. He suddenly felt cold, spikes of ice flowing in his arms instead of warm blood. He fought to react – to cry out to his mother. Water gushed from his mouth, and he was suddenly yanked upwards.

Cosmo choked, and vomited heaving gouts of liquid as his lungs involuntarily convulsed. He could feel a slap on his face and tried to open his eyes but they would not at once obey. He gasped – each time air came in it went out with water. He was about to black out again when he was finally able to get a single full breath. He coughed and coughed, barely slitting open red sore eyes through a hammering headache that wracked through his temples and his ears.

"Cosmo!" Saira pleaded, right in front of his face. "Cosmo – say something!"

"I'm–" he coughed again, spitting water that just seemed to keep coming. "I'm try–"

"He will live," Kaiden's strong voice came through. "He must breathe."

"Cosmo you almost drowned!" Saira yelped at him. "Oh Cosmo you scared me!" He was crushed against the cold wet folds of fabric of her chest, and he went limp – just focusing on getting his breathing to normalize. He couldn't see anything anyway.

"We must move," Kaiden said in a gravelly voice. "The shore is bad. Gorig will come."

Saira sat Cosmo up and held his face in her hands – her warmth something he felt he could melt into for a moment. Every muscle in his body felt empty, as if they had been completely drained of all life. The memory of his dream flashed and he moaned. "Mother..." He coughed and coughed and could not stop himself from emitting low moans.

"Sssh. Sshh, oh Cosmo, it's all right. We're all right. Kaiden saved us. He saved me – then he saved you. We're all right now."

"We must move," Kaiden repeated, a change to the same type of impatience Cosmo had heard the first time they'd met. "Away and to the crags. We cannot stay – they have heard and will come now." He easily lifted Cosmo in his strong arms and immediately started taking long strides uphill, away from the lake edge.

"Don't – don't we want others to come?" Saira protested. She had to jog to keep up. "Don't we want help?"

"Gorig will not help," Kaiden replied.

"Gow rig?" Saira queried, out of breath as she approximated the word and hurried to follow Kaiden's path away from the lake. He walked as if Cosmo was weightless. "Is that another tribe?"

"Gorig. No. Simple animals. They are in the forest. Very large. Wild. Very wild – they are big, strong and... mean. They will kill us if they can."

Cosmo could suddenly feel the closeness of the rocks and trees as they passed. He was dizzy, and kept spitting up water. His headache pounded in his temples, and the one time he managed to slit open his reddened bleary eyes he saw hard sheer rock walls extending up around him.

"Where... where are we? Where is the ship?"

"Gone," Kaiden said bluntly.

"They... they need to..." he started to protest, forcing his mind to think of the next necessary step – rescue. But his breathing demanded his concentration and it seemed to take all his remaining effort if he moved his mouth to speak.

"Cosmo?" Saira exclaimed, reaching out to touch his face as Kaiden walked.

"He breathes. He will get better," Kaiden explained to her through his own stilted breaths.

You'll get better... Cosmo heard his mother's voice in his head. He tried to imagine her face, but was struck hard in the nose with a thick raindrop of water. He blinked his eyes open and was immediately hit by another drop on his face. The blurred clouds above them seemed dark and full. He brought his hand up to his face to wipe away the water and suddenly realized his glasses were gone.

"My- My glasses!" his eyes looked around frantically and he started to seize up in Kaiden's arms. Kaiden growled slightly at the jerking movement as he walked, and Cosmo became still. He closed his eyes as a sinking feeling drew over him from the loss.

"Kaiden, don't we need to find shelter?" Saira asked as she jogged alongside them. More raindrops came down on them.

"We are already wet. The rain will mask our... smell," he answered curtly. His breathing was starting to labor from carrying Cosmo, and his face had grown into a frown.

"Put me down," Cosmo asked. "I'm too heavy."

"No," Kaiden answered quickly with a huff. "You will be slow. We cannot be slow. The rocks here are only crags. We must find a big... hole. A hole to hide in. Gorig are coming."

Cosmo craned his head to look at the princess. Her wide eyes tried to take in as much as they could of where they were going as Kaiden led them through the thickening rain.

fourteen

Ogren dragged himself up the jagged rocks at the lake's edge, coughing and spitting water. Once he was onto a large slab of bedrock he collapsed face down and heaved for breath. After a moment he growled and reached underneath himself and struggled to pull the spike gun from his sopping wet pants. Smacking it down to his right, he pulled in his arms tightly to his chest underneath himself and tried to recover some warmth.

He'd barely been able to think, much less plan, before he'd had to jump the two hundred or so feet from the ship. The lake was small, and if he had waited another second he would have jumped out onto rocks. Barely able to swim, once in the water he had quickly realized he had to unclasp his heavy cloak and let it go, or it would have drowned him.

It was perfect, he thought as he brought his forehead down to rest against the cold stone. *It was so perfect. How did I mess that up?*

The ropes had worked much better than he had planned – the princess and the others had been taken totally by surprise and barely made a sound before they'd passed over and below the side of the ship. Nobody on board had heard and come running. All they had to do was fall down onto the rocks and die. He could have hidden on board the ship and nobody would ever have known what had happened to them, or even where to look. He cursed as he winced his eyes shut, and rolled over to allow himself to breathe and think. He wiped the wet flop of his half-head of hair from the left side of his face. The sun was beginning to set and the sky was darkening.

I'm alone. I'm literally in the middle of nowhere and I'm alone. He gritted his teeth then opened his eyes, staring up into the gathering gray clouds. The ship had passed on and away towards its destination, apparently totally unaware of the brief drama that had occurred at the edge of its deck.

The puny attendant had seen his face, stared straight into it. So he had to die. The princess and the attendant. And probably the jungle rube as well, if he couldn't find a way to frame him for the deaths.

Ogren realized he'd lost his knife somehow in the drop into the lake. He reached out beside himself and felt for the pistol, grabbed it and brought it up to lie on top of his chest, holding it tightly. *Two shots. Not enough.*

Then... what? Walk the way back? How could he possibly do that and survive? It was incredibly far, and he'd have to get past the dead zone. Crossing that was supposed to be impossible. He had his hip flask for a small trifle of water, but that was it.

They'll come looking for her, he thought to himself, working through the argument in his head and letting himself relax. *They won't find her but they'll find me.* He'd have to make up some story – wandering the wilderness. Or some other ship that had crashed into the lake. *Or something.*

With heaving breaths, he sat up and stared off down the lake towards where he'd seen his three targets hit the water. They were nowhere in sight, but he could see a break in the rocks where they had probably gone for shelter. Forcing himself to stand up, he clutched at his pistol and coughed violently before staggering up the shore towards rocks that rose vertically near the edge.

He heard motion in the bushes and stopped, squinting and listening. An uneasy fear crept up his back as he carefully raised his pistol and flicked the power switch on its side. Nothing happened. His eyes widened and he glared at the pistol before he struck it with the palm of his hand. He shook it and heavy drops of water flicked from its end. *It's wet. Probably no good when it's wet.* He turned the power switch off but still pointed the useless gun at the bushes. He backed up slowly along the edge of the lake, then quickened his pace to a trot as he moved away from the spot where he'd come out of the water. *Find them,* he thought. *Find them and kill them, then worry about what's next.*

He was sure he could see gleaming black eyes that stared from the foliage, and felt like something followed his movement along the shoreline and towards the walls of sharp rocks that ringed the lake.

Ogren shoved his gun into his pants and cursed as he tried to climb, fingertips desperately clinging to the side of the sheer crags. As he drew himself up the incline the smell reached him – a musky scent he'd never experienced before. Wafting into his nose he suddenly blew out his breath and scrunched up his face in disgust. "Holy crap," he muttered, glancing around and back towards the shore. "What the hell is that?"

He tried to force the experience from his mind and concentrate only on making it to the top of the rocks, onto a small hill. Once he achieved this he drew the gun out of his pants again and desperately flicked the power switch back and forth. A strong electronic beep was emitted, and two green lights on the side of the pistol slowly illuminated, one after the other. Ogren sighed in relief. *Back in business.*

He raised the gun and looked around at his surroundings on the top of the hill. On the edge he could see back down where he had come to the lake, as well as down a short incline to the edge of a thick forest. *Fine.* He sat down and put the gun in his lap, then wrapped his arms around his chest to warm up. At least from the top of the mound he could see where he needed to go. *Now, take a minute to make a plan...*

He heard a clear chirping noise from the forest, and his eyes shot wide open as he fumbled for the pistol in his lap. As he scanned the brush he suddenly heard a low growl from behind him, where he had come up from the lake. He whirled around, stumbled up from his seated position and waved the gun in the direction of the noise. After only a moment he realized he was not looking in the direction of the forest – a much simpler and easier way to approach his position. *The growl was to distract me!* He twisted about again, cursing to bring the barrel of his weapon to bear on the foliage in front of him.

A heavy raindrop smacked into the bald side of his head, bouncing off and dribbling down his face. Another hit his shoulder, and then a third hit the barrel of his gun. *Oh, wonderful.* More raindrops quickly followed, thick and heavy. Ogren grimaced and squinted towards the forest in the dying light of the evening that still managed to thrust its way through the dark gray clouds.

The stench suddenly rolled across where he stood and filled his nose. He coughed and gagged, trying to breathe through his mouth as a terror started to creep its way up his spine. A chuckling chirp came from his left, then another from his right. He waved his gun erratically in the direction of each, and had to work hard to keep himself from pulling the trigger as his heart pounded in his chest.

This is bad. They can see me, and I can't see them. His eyes darted around and he swiveled his head, trying to catch movement. It was like some of the less-than-intelligent plans he'd heard in the slums of Carnarvon. Usually involving someone sacrificing themselves and the rest of the crowd then getting whatever goods were to be got. Perfect plan until it came to choosing who was going to die – volunteers were hard to find.

"First one of you is gonna die at least!" he barked off towards the trees. He trained the gun around, squinting into the dark and the rain. "Who's that gonna be?!"

My plan's not much better, he admitted to himself. *Gotta move. I'm giving them time to work it out.* Any direction was better than staying still in plain sight.

He suddenly hopped a step down the slope, off to the right in the direction of the end of the lake Kaiden, Saira and Cosmo had fallen into. He held the gun out in front of himself and swung it purposefully back and forth, striding hurriedly while trying to keep his eyes wide open through the constant raindrops. Twice he could feel a terror swell in his chest that tightened his finger around the trigger of the gun, but he was able to keep his head and avoided wasting a shot.

Ogren made his way toward a long patch of sharp rocks and smaller rounded boulders, away from the trees and brush. He instantly felt proud of his decision – he could see around himself much more clearly and had managed to escape the prison of the small hill without being attacked. The tall sharp rocks soon gave way to cracked stone walls edged in small gravel and sand, with tufts of foliage sticking out of holes. *A cave,* he thought. *I need a cave, or an alcove. Something to sit in with only one way out.* As he thought of a sanctuary he was caught by a wave of fatigue, which caused him to feel his heart drop in his chest. *One way out, but I'm still gonna have to stay awake.* His back and neck ached from exertion, and he felt a chill of hopelessness tingle in his skin.

A sudden loud growl ahead of him made him stagger to a stop, and he yanked the spike gun up to point at level in front of himself. As soon as he did two chirping noises came from each side, slightly behind him. He instinctively flicked his head to the left and the right to try to find the source of the chirping, but quickly gave up. The fear he was experiencing made his shoulders begin to shake. He swallowed hard and looked around for something to put his back against. Then he saw the hole – a sliver in the stone wall face mere inches wide. *Big enough?*

The smell of the beasts tracking him rolled into his nostrils and his mind shouted its response – *big enough!* He scrambled towards the rock wall and thrust a shoulder into the cranny. It took all his effort to get the depth of his chest to fit but he strained and managed to work himself forwards, head rotated to look back towards the opening. He pushed and pushed, working his body further until he was more than an arm's length inside. Luckily, his hand that held the gun was on the side of the opening he had wedged himself into. He raised it and stared at the gray of the night that was exposed through the crack of the entrance. He watched water drip from the end of the barrel of his gun, realizing that now in the dark he couldn't see much further beyond that. The shaking in his chest made his breathing erratic as he angrily called out to his pursuers.

"Come get me, you stinky buggers!"

A dark shape flitted past the crack, and in his terror Ogren instinctively fired the gun.

Spike guns were not subtle – a huge flash burst from the muzzle, and a booming crack thudded through the fissure Ogren had crammed himself into and rolled out into the forest. The pain of the light on his eyes made him wince them shut and the searing of the sound on his eardrums overwhelmed him for a moment. He shakily emitted a loud curse at his own stupidity, and waited to recover his hearing through the ringing in his ears.

A shadow fell across his face, which drove him to awkwardly rotate his twisted neck to look upwards. Above him through the raindrops he could see a slit of the sky and a dark shape looking down. He had to cough through the stench in the air, and huffed for breath.

Wedged between the sheer rock walls, rain poured down on him as the dark shapes simply watched. Waiting.

fifteen

"What was that?!" Saira exclaimed.

Cosmo, Saira and Kaiden all sat in the darkness of an alcove, pressed low against the rocks over a stone lip that shielded them from the outside. All three of them had wide eyes as they listened to the fading reverberations of the loud crack that had pierced the air through the sound of the rain.

"That wasn't lightning," Cosmo stated flatly. "That was something... I don't know. Like a gun shot."

"That was not sound of forest," Kaiden agreed. "Metal. Metal... breaking. Coming apart – uh, cracking. Like a wood crack in fire. Coming apart quickly."

"Exploding? Couldn't be. What is made of metal in a forest?" Cosmo asked, skeptical. "Do the Gorig use it?"

"No, no tools," Kaiden explained.

They had managed to find the small cave-like hole among the crags a few minutes' walk from the lake's edge. At first Saira didn't know what Kaiden meant when he motioned towards a rock overhang, but once she got close enough she was able to make it out – an entrance under the lip. Slightly up from the ground, it was well concealed and deep enough to hold all three of them comfortably. Cosmo had been irritated enough that he'd had to be carried, and was grateful to get out of the thickening downpour.

"Is it someone looking for us? A signal?" Saira asked hopefully. "Maybe the ship turned around!"

"We should go find out," Cosmo agreed.

"No. It is dark. Gorig are near. I will go. You must stay here in... hole?"

"Cave," Saira corrected.

"Is it a cave or a tunnel?" Cosmo asked, looking back into the cold darkness behind them.

"Cave." Kaiden spoke the word slowly and listened to his own voice as he did, to make sure the sound was right. "There is rock all around. But you cannot see," he finished in a flat, dismissive voice.

"No, I can't see," Cosmo huffed at the tone. "Not without my glasses, anyway. And not in this pitch black." He jutted his chin in the direction of Saira's voice. "She might be able to."

"No, I can't see anything in here either," Saira countered. "Once we came in I had to hold Kaiden's robe until he put you down."

"I am sorry, Mister Cosmo. I did not mean my words to offend you. I did mean my words to saying your eyes are...

wrong. Uh– different." From his voice they could tell he was anxiously searching for an explanation that he felt made sense in their language. "They do not... work... here. They are changed, by Masters."

"Probably to look more normal to them. More what the Masters looked like," Saira added. "I guess they didn't really need to see in the dark."

"I will go," Kaiden said, with his voice already receding.

Cosmo reached out around himself and found Saira's arm, then adjusted his position and brought himself closer to her. He suddenly felt her hand pat up his chest and rest on his cheek. "I'm so glad you're ok," she said softly. "Kaiden saved your life. After he saved mine."

He raised his own hand to find her cheek as well, and they sat for a moment, letting their touch work to calm them since their eyes could not. He could feel the shape of her face and tell her expression.

"I don't know why you're smiling," Cosmo stated bemusedly. "Somebody just tried to kill you for the second time."

Saira's smile drained from her face and she pulled herself away from him, hand and face. "Thank you for reminding me," she said in an irritated tone.

"Sorry," he mumbled. "I shouldn't have brought it up." Cosmo could hear her rearrange her position – probably to draw her knees up and arms around herself in protection.

"I saw the Human on the boat," she said. "When we fell. When I was just hanging there I looked up and saw him standing above you. The one with the... hair on half his head."

"I saw him too," Cosmo agreed. "I'd know him if I saw him again. Hair or not." He realized he already missed the feel of her hand on his face. "I- I really am sorry."

"It's fine. I'm not mad at you.." her voice trailed off, before she added ".. much."

"What?" Cosmo was incredulous. "What did I do?"

"Your little comment on the ship. That I don't listen to you anymore."

"Well it certainly seems like it," he protested.

"Not fair," she returned. "What am I supposed to do? I can't listen to you telling me what to do for the rest of my life. My father has always told me that I need to make my own decisions. Cosmo – even you tell me that!"

"Intelligent, informed decisions," Cosmo amended. "Not ones made in haste that are just for the thrill of the moment. I-"

"Sometimes the thrill of the moment is what I'm about! Cosmo were you ever my age?"

Cosmo was silent for a moment in the dark. "No. I don't remember ever being your age," he said quietly. "I remember being younger than you. I remember... my mother. I remember being a child. But I never..." he trailed off.

He felt Saira's hand on his face again. He closed his eyes and let himself feel the connection, trying to think of what to say. "I never had... a tawdry fling on a passing fancy."

Saira snickered.

Cosmo smiled, then sighed and decided to continue for her amusement. "I never drank myself silly, or... ran off into the black of night stark naked with a great big smile on my face."

Saira laughed and he smiled even more at the sound. "You can still do those things, you know?" she said.

"What, you're going to teach me how to be reckless?"

"I'm not reck-!" she blurted loudly, before cutting herself off and lowering her voice to a heated whisper. She withdrew her hand from his face again, indignant. "I'm not reckless! I know what I'm doing!"

"Mmmm... you know what you've done after you've done it," he said plainly. "Not sure you've thought about what's going to happen when you start doing something."

Saira huffed. "Really?! Really, that's what you think of me? I'm that big of a disappointment to you?"

Cosmo's throat constricted and he felt a sudden sinking feeling in his stomach. He swallowed hard and felt the burning in his cheeks. *Too far,* he thought. *I went too far.*

"I'm sorry," he said after a moment. "I- You... you've gotten better. I mean... than you were..." He stopped himself. *Not helping.*

Saira let her silence speak for her.

"Gorig," Kaiden's voice came suddenly from the darkness. "Gorig are close." Cosmo hadn't heard him approach at all – it was as if he'd just appeared out of nowhere beside them. He also had no idea how long Kaiden had been there – had he heard their angry interchange?

"I thought you said Gorig don't use-"

"No. Something else is there. They hunt it."

Cosmo sniffed and rubbed his nose. Something suddenly smelled wrong. He blew breath out his nose and inhaled through it. Was it Kaiden? The aboriginal Felid had smelled quite pleasant earlier, Cosmo was sure of it. But this wasn't a Felid smell at all. "Do you smell some-"

"It is Gorig," Kaiden said with a sigh. "I am sorry Mister Cosmo. I touch a tree with my arm. The Gorig also touch tree. It is their smell."

"That's terrible!" Saira exclaimed. Cosmo could tell she was holding something over her nose. "I didn't know what it was."

"Well, at least we know where they are if they smell like that," Cosmo said. "What were they hunting?"

"I did not get close enough. I could not tell."

"Hopefully just some animal – their dinner or something," Saira suggested. "The sound must have been whatever they were chasing."

They sat in near silence for more than a minute. Cosmo listened to the patter of the rain outside, but his mind went back to his conversation with the princess. *I'm that big a disappointment to you?* kept playing over and over in his head.

"Mister Cosmo, what is word 'reckless'?" Kaiden asked curiously after a few minutes of silence.

Oh crap, Cosmo thought. *He heard. He probably heard the whole thing.* He could feel his cheeks heat up in embarrassment.

Saira sighed loudly, openly embarrassed. Cosmo cringed at what he imagined her face must look like. "Uh... it...", he started with a quaver.

"It is when a person acts without thinking," Saira said loudly and firmly. "They are inconsiderate and rude. They don't care how other people are going to feel about what they do."

"I see," Kaiden said quickly, then went silent.

Cosmo's breath shuddered and he tried wildly to think of what to say. He couldn't have Kaiden think that description was his proper opinion of the princess. "Kaiden, I don't think the princess is reckless", he started, trying hard to sound sincere. "She and I both know that. I was... I was-"

"We are sorry, Kaiden," Saira finished for him, changing her voice to sound serious and diplomatic. "We didn't know you were there and that you had heard us. We... quarrel some times. I mean well, and Cosmo means well, but..."

"Sometimes we say things that we feel in the moment, but do not really mean," Cosmo added, finally finding something to say.

"We have this," Kaiden responded, also trying to soothe the tension. "We have a saying for it."

"What is that?" Cosmo queried, eager to get past the apologies.

"*Pagh Ebbet*," he answered. "It means 'your tail is talking."

Saira chuckled. "As yes, you were saying that your tails seem to think for themselves."

"Does your tail speak often, Kaiden?" Cosmo asked with a smile.

Kaiden laughed and Cosmo relaxed, feeling happy that they had reached a comfortable understanding.

"Jalendra would say yes…" he started, but the aboriginal Felid's voice trailed off.

"I am looking forward to meeting this Jalendra," Cosmo said. In the blackness of the cave he turned his head so that his voice was directed more at where he knew the princess sat. But it was clear he was still speaking to the ambassador. "You mentioned her before. She must be a big part of your life."

Saira was completely silent.

"Yes…" Kaiden said softly, but did not elaborate.

They sat in the dark and listened to the rain.

sixteen

Jalendra sat in the dim light of the fire inside the warriors' den, staring into the embers and inhaling the pungent smoke that filled the hut. She had sat there a long time – not knowing what to do with herself. She knew that night had probably come, and still she had not seen or heard from Kem. Even if he had appeared, she had no idea what they would do after what had happened. Maybe he didn't either. How would they salvage her training so she could reach her destiny? What was her destiny?

She was brought sweet water and a thick gruel, but tasted neither of them. She just sat and waited miserably, until finally she heard a commotion and saw some of the other warrior trainees running to the entrance of the den. It then became very quiet, and Jalendra heard the soft padfalls of a larger Felid approach her. Not a warrior. *Here in the den?* She turned to see Maresh, the healer Pilla.

The older female smiled and stooped to sit beside Jalendra, graciously but uncomfortably. She did not face the fire – knowing that the warriors' pride taught them to protect the purity of their flames from the eyes of outsiders. The plump female with gray misted fur always wore what seemed to be too many layers of tough cloth. Jalendra figured it was so that she could always lend one to another. Maresh's smile was warm and inviting, and she never seemed to be anxious, even when there were many injuries to tend to. "Kem asked me to see you," she said, explaining her presence. "You have been in here for a long time, and I felt I must intrude. You have injuries?"

Jalendra blinked in surprise. *My shoulders?* She glanced at them. Kem would not have bothered to call a healer, particularly the village Pilla, for such a trivial injury. She had endured much worse in training and had not required any salves or bandage. "I have fought. But I am well, Pilla Maresh. Perhaps you have misheard-"

"Ah, well," Maresh said, leaning forward to cluck her tongue softly as she brushed her eyes past the tops of the young warrior's arms. "Yes, nothing serious. A misunderstanding on my part, then. I apologize for the transgression. If there is nothing else..." her voice trailed off and she cocked a brow. But after only a short moment she leaned to her left to rock herself, intending to move her bulk up to standing again.

"Maresh, I-"

"Yes, child?" Maresh stopped and leaned forward, looking into the young warrior's face.

"Do healers have... a power? Fire... inside?"

"Fire?", Maresh queried, face slightly askew.

"Yes, flames of a fire. Kem calls them the flames of your destiny. Your hearth," she said, looking back into the flickering embers of the real fire in front of them. "The base of who you are meant to be."

Maresh sighed and looked thoughtfully at Jalendra. "No. Not like what I've heard the warriors speak of, for their... killing power. We learn and teach our knowledge. Improve our salves and bindings for the body, and ways of thinking for the mind. But fire, no. That has not been in the nature of a healer's path for a thousand cycles."

Jalendra looked away from the fire suddenly, brows up. "But it was once...?"

"Yes, before the scarring of the planet," Maresh sighed. "Before that, the warriors and the healers were not very different in terms of what they could do with life. It is said when in harmony with the planet they could take it or they could give it."

"What happened to them? To their power?"

Maresh was quiet for a moment before answering, as if thinking back on a painful memory. "The fire in the sky, the shaking of the ground. The black death cut into the planet. You know what I speak of?"

"Yes, I know. I have been to the Teeth of the Forest."

Maresh nodded. "The healers – all of our kind with what you call 'fire'. They went to... the injury, in the skin of the planet. They all went together. None of them returned."

"Why?"

The healer Pilla closed her eyes for a moment, moving her hands on top of each other and on top of her chest. "A healer cannot heal what is dead – they can only take what life is there and make it flourish, make it renew. What I have heard said by my Pilla, when I was young, was that the fire that is given to stoke life is difficult to replace. That some parts of the... healer... are changed. Removed, or damaged. So... those that went to heal the planet gave all the fire they had in themselves. But the injury was too great. Their power was not enough, and they were destroyed."

Jalendra was silent, more questions brimming in her mind. She didn't know where to start. *Kem sent Maresh here,* she thought. *He didn't know what else to do.* As Pilla he would know the same secrets and history Maresh knew. This must have been the only thing he could think of. She turned to the hearth in front of them and stared at it for a moment, before she realized that fear was holding her back from accepting what she knew.

"Maresh, I...", she faltered, closing her eyes.

"Your fire is not that which kills," Maresh said quickly.

"No," she admitted. "I mean- yes... I have that. I can do that but..."

"Your power is more. Deeper."

"I don't know," Jalendra said as she slowly shook her head. She turned and opened her eyes to look into Maresh's face.

The older female was smiling calmly, but the light danced in her eyes. "If you believe your fire is your destiny, maybe you should find out."

"What does that make me? I can kill. I have the warrior's power, the warriors training. Since I was a child I... Master Kem. He is my master. But he doesn't know... even you don't know. And you say nobody knows-"

"It's all right. It's all right child," Maresh soothed. She placed a hand gently on Jalendra's leg. "It will come. Be who you are and it will come. You don't need to try to change."

With Maresh's hand on her body and the calming words, Jalendra could feel the anxiety quickly disappearing from her body and mind. The questions remained, but they were calm and ordered. *Is this what I'm meant to do - what she is doing now? All I know how to do is to hunt, to fight, to kill. Has all that been a waste?*

A young boy darted in front of them, and reached by the fire to grab a ceremonial sash and spear. Maresh drew back, not wanting to get in the way. Jalendra's mind was broken from her stream of questions and she put out her hand to stop him. "What is it, Vash? Why do you run? What is happening?"

"Pilla Mares, Honored Jalendra," he said quickly as he bowed. "A princess from the north is arriving. We have been told to be ready to greet her."

"But she's not due for five days," Jalendra shook her head at the boy. "Kaiden is travelling with her, he's bringing her here."

"Yes, but they are arriving very soon – this dawn," Maresh finished for the boy. "Not in five days. I was told it was not expected. The Pilla have decided we must try to greet her properly. Is there some problem we do not know of?"

Jalendra blinked in surprise and shook her head. She let go of the boy but then looked back at the embers of the fire. She found herself cracking a smile – at least she would be able to talk to Kaiden about what had happened. He would be happy – there was now something other than himself that his father had been wrong about.

She stood and helped Maresh to do the same, bowing to the Pilla. "I will seek your counsel," she said. "After Kaiden's return. I have... many questions. Those that Master Kem cannot answer."

"And some I will not be able to answer. But some I can..." Maresh graciously returned the bow with a broad smile, turned and strode to the entrance of the hut. Jalendra followed her, but stopped for a moment to rinse her hands and arms in a small cleaning bowl by the entrance. As she moved outside into the late evening, she could hear the very low hum of power sails of a ship far off in the distance. Near the pathway to the ship dock the providers were lining up their wares in a row for display to impress the princess.

She looked all around her as her people scurried and made impromptu preparations, and chuckled as she thought of Kaiden approaching with the princess. *Hard for your father to ignore the attention the village is giving you now!*

seventeen

Ogren awoke to the strong stench in the air, with the flop of his wet hair pasted down over the left side of his face. He grimaced and tried to move his legs, but they were numb and wedged underneath him. He moaned and pulled his face away from the rock wall he had fallen asleep against, feeling the bite of pain from circulation as it was restored to his cheek.

I'm still alive, he thought as he slit his eyes open and tried to focus on his predicament. In the dim light gathering before dawn, through the gap of the entrance to his crag he could only see trees. One tree had a huge black scar on it, and burn marks from where the hot spike from his gun had impaled its trunk and exploded into hot splinters of molten metal.

He took a deep breath and grunted as he worked to free his legs, and shimmy along the rock in front of him towards the entrance to the crack. He stopped just before the opening and listened – but all he could hear was the rustling of the trees in the wind. *They better be gone,* he thought. *Or this is going to be a short excursion.*

He poked his head out and quickly glanced left and right, but could make out nothing but rocks, boulders, and shrubs leading up to the trees. A sigh of relief, and he pulled himself fully from the fissure in the rock, shaking out his legs to try to restore circulation to them. He was still soaking wet, and shivered as the wind blew past him. He raised his hand holding the gun and looked at the single green light left on its side. *One left - one spike, three targets.* He frowned and thought for a moment, the memory of the previous night weighing heavily on him as he tried to think about a plan. *I'm gonna need the gun just to survive the way back.* He growled in frustration - strangling people was so much more work than shooting them. And fighting the aboriginal was certainly an unknown. He knew he could take the princess' attendant and the princess, even both at the same time if he needed to. But the aboriginal... maybe use the spike on him?

His hands began to shake involuntarily. He turned the pistol off and shoved it into his waistband, then pulled his arms close across his chest for warmth. *I need to eat and drink,* he thought. *I'm not going to last long otherwise.*

He started to walk towards the trees, thinking he would have to trap or shoot something he could eat. *How do I trap something? How do I cook it?* He didn't know how to start a fire either. The severity of his situation drew across his weary mind and he could feel himself start to panic. He clenched his teeth and forced himself to think of his next step – just the one right in front of him. Water.

He started to walk, towards the lake but also around it. Some kind of stream must empty into or out of the lake somewhere. Especially after the rain, the overflow on the body of water meant there should be fresh running water somewhere nearby.

If I run into those three so much the better.

eighteen

Jalendra walked down with the other villagers towards the dock that would receive the ship. She could picture in her mind Kaiden's face when they'd said their goodbyes, and now found herself smiling at the memory. She spied Landu the provider Pilla standing and talking with Maresh, and a few feet away from them she saw Kem's back. The warrior stood stiffly watching the dim line of the horizon and the blinking lights of the approaching ship.

She came towards the three Pilla somewhat awkwardly, as she did not know what Kem had told the others. Nor did she know how Kem was going to react, now that he had had some time to process what had happened.

"Good morning, Jalendra," Maresh said with a smile, as if they had not just been talking. Landu did not greet her, and simply wrung his hands and looked around at the preparations being made, obviously upset at the lack of time that he had been given.

"They are almost here?" she inquired as she looked off at the lights, unsure of how bright they would get as it neared the village. She could hear the hum of the power sails – certainly not the largest she'd ever heard but still enough to softly throb the air from a distance.

"Oh yes," Maresh looked at her with a smile. "Nothing to be upset about," her voice soothed. "Just a small change in plans."

"Hardly," Landu grumbled.

Maresh looked annoyed at Landu for a moment, but quickly turned her focus back to Jalendra. "My dear, Master Kem is just there. The ship is about to arrive – perhaps you would like to stand with him now? Then all will be ready."

Jalendra bowed and took a few steps to her place standing next to Kem as the vibrations from the power sails started to saturate the air. The floating ships that coasted not far abover the ground were a rarity in the southern villages, and regardless of the occasion everyone usually stopped what they were doing to marvel at them. Kem did not take his eyes off the *Daedalus* as it came fully into view and coasted down quickly towards the wood pilings of the aboriginal's makeshift sky boat dock.

"This is wrong," Kem growled.

"Can we talk about this later please, Master?" Jalendra said, swallowing as she blew out her breath.

He did not turn to her. Instead he broke the line of people waiting for the ship, took two steps forward and jumped, running to the dock before the ship had even touched down. With his powerful legs he bypassed all the stairs and leapt up onto the rough wooden pilings.

"Kem!" Maresh yelped. Jalendra was perplexed – but then she saw the motion on the deck. An Impalan in a wide hat waving his arms back and forth.

"Something is wrong!" she yelped at Maresh and Landu, and then surged forward to follow her master. With the exception of Kem, Jalendra was faster than anyone in the village. She ran down the same way Kem had gone and mirrored his leap towards the ship. Rope lines came down as the ship moved over the dock, and two deckhands deftly slid down them to drop firmly onto the ground.

"*Ky don et mah?*" Kem said loudly in the aboriginal language – the only one that he knew. *What is wrong?* One of the deckhands ignored him and started to tie down lines that would stabilize the ship. The other quickly tapped his lips with fingers and shook his head in exaggeration to denote his lack of ability to speak the same language, then grabbed a guide line and started to fasten it to the dock.

Kem grimaced and his eyes blazed in frustration. The ship was gradually sinking down towards the pilings that would hold it, but impatiently he grabbed the rope that the deckhand had slid down and immediately started to raise himself, his wiry muscles making quick work of the climb.

Jalendra surged for the second drop line, mirroring her master's intent to get up to the ship deck.

As she came over the top of the ship railing, other deck hands started to open up the gang plank area and strike some of the steering sails. The vibrations in the air thudded hard for a moment as the ship slowly rested onto the creaking wooden dock beams, and then quickly settled down to a subtle hum as the engines rested from their task of keeping the ship in the air.

As Jalendra approached, she could tell Kem was already trying to communicate with the Impalan ship captain, using hand gestures and grunts and bits of the aboriginal language he thought the male might understand.

"*Cor ah den-te? COR AH?!*" Kem said loudly, as if the volume of his voice might make his words somehow understandable. *Where are they? WHERE?* Captain Fasil looked fraught with fear – he could not understand Kem either. The male swallowed hard and his face was red with his own frustration and embarrassment.

Jalendra thought hard for the words to use. "Where Kaiden?" she blurted. The captain's eyes flashed and he looked at her in hope – words he recognized.

"Lost!" Fasil exclaimed, looking at her. "They done disappeared! We thought they was in the cabins, but we went ta rouse 'em few minutes ago and they ain't there!"

Kem scrunched up his face in confusion and anger. "*Ky don 'lost' et emi?*" he barked, turning to look at Jalendra. *What does 'lost' mean?*

"Lost... *t- tetray*" Jalendra stammered, trying to remember the bits of the language that Kaiden had taught her. "*Tetray – Ki na vod cor ah den te*", she said to Kem. *Lost – he doesn't know where they are.*

"Kem!" Maresh called from the top of the gang plank. Landu and Maresh both stood there in confusion, eyes flicking back and forth from the captain to Jalendra to Kem. "*Ky ah vet?*" she said loudly in irritation. *What is happening?*

Kem moved to stomp towards Maresh and Landu. Jalendra followed but felt the barrier instilled in her upbringing that told her it was forbidden to listen to the Pilla's private conversations. Her heart thudded in concern for Kaiden, and she could not stop herself from straining to hear what they said.

"Lost. They lost them," Kem said angrily.

"What does that mean?" Landu queried. "How do you lose someone on a sky boat?"

Maresh looked confused as well. "Did they stop anywhere?" It seemed incredulous to her that this would happen and that somehow the ship would leave without them.

Captain Fasil came up and stood beside Jalendra, also eagerly trying to catch part of the conversation even though he could not follow the language. He looked back and forth from Jalendra to the Pilla.

"It is likely they fell from the ship," Kem grumbled. "Kaiden must have done something foolish to try to impress the princess."

"Kem," Maresh growled back in irritation. "Despite the fact that he is your son, he is quite intelligent," she chided. "He knows their language and impressed them enough to let him bring their princess to us. I doubt your assessment of his 'foolishness' is accurate in this instance."

"Arguing isn't helping," Landu muttered in exasperation. "Who else knows their language?"

"Jalendra knows some words. I will go with her on the ship and find them," Kem grumbled after a moment. "Now. Agreed?"

"Yes," Maresh responded. Landu nodded quickly and turned to walk back down the gang plank. Maresh paused and looked at Kem as he walked towards Jalendra and the captain.

"*Ket et verr, a fett rah*" Ken said to Fasil, avoiding Jalendra's eyes. *Take me back where you came, to find them.*

The captain gulped, confused. "I don't know what ye'r sayin'. You want us ta stay here? You wanna comm with the king 'n call in the Navy? What?"

Gritting his teeth, Kem angrily pointed at his eyes then swept his arm in an arc, hand extended in a gesture towards where the ship had come from.

"Find," Jalendra injected. "We find. Kaiden lost, we find."

"Ah. Find 'em. Fine. Yep." The male immediately turned towards the other sailor on the deck and started to bark commands to undo the moorings and reverse the process they had just completed to dock the ship.

"I need you," Kem said to Jalendra. "To talk to them. Otherwise you would stay here."

She stared into his face, then glanced past him towards Maresh. The healer Pilla had stood still at the top of the gang plank, waiting to see what Jalendra would choose to do on her own. "No."

Kem's brows furrowed in annoyance.

"I would go even if you didn't need me."

She looked to Maresh and shook her head once. The healer Pilla nodded in understanding, and immediately turned to descend the plank to the ground.

Jalendra turned away from Kem, walking through the confusing rush of deckhands preparing the ship for departure.

nineteen

As the day broke and the sky lightened, Cosmo, Saira and Kaiden cautiously emerged from their rocky den. Clothing still damp and hair mottled, Saira drew her cloak tightly around herself and shivered. Kaiden's face looked grim and he sniffed the air to test it for signature scents of danger.

"We need to eat something," Cosmo said. "And drink clean water. We're not going to have energy to move anywhere unless we eat."

"Yes Mister Cosmo. I will find... fruit. And plant." Kaiden said quietly but with a disappointed face. "No meat here. Gorig will hear or smell if I kill. It is danger here. We will move away today."

"Danger, yes." Cosmo gulped and moved to brush up against the princess. She frowned in discomfort from their long night in the rock but stayed next to him for warmth.

"I need to pee," Saira whispered to him. "How do I tell him that without embarrassing him? Or me?"

Cosmo turned to look at Kaiden. "She needs to pee."

Saira sighed and rolled her eyes.

"Ah, yes. I am sorry," Kaiden smiled uncomfortably. "That should have been my think. I will find safe place for you, then get the food." He moved away towards the rock face and then disappeared around the corner of a pile of boulders.

"Thank you," Saira said quietly to Cosmo. "Very diplomatic." She stood still and continued to hold herself for warmth.

Cosmo shuddered as a breeze blew past and Saira quickly moved to open her cloak and draw him inside of it. He sighed and stood pressed up against her so they could share body heat.

"You're taking care of me now?" he asked in bemusement.

He could feel the tension rise in her body and the sigh in her breath as she decided how to respond. "Somebody has to, so you know what it's like."

"I'm sorry," he said. "I'm sorry for what I said last night." She relaxed slightly and he felt encouraged. "This isn't my place, out here. Isn't my life or what I'm used to. It's not even what I want to be used to. And you – you being... in charge of yourself. That's not what I'm used to either."

"What do you want to be used to?" She asked.

"My... our home. Doing what I know. Being safe. And you being safe. Me knowing you're safe."

"I'm not always going to be safe, Cosmo. That's life. I know that may seem reckless to you, but..."

"I know," he sighed. "You have to grow and change, and so do I. I just... I guess I haven't been ready for that."

They were both silent for a minute. He moved his arm to embrace her and so they could gather more warmth from each other.

"Cosmo, I don't know what's going to happen. But I want to find out. I'm excited to find out," she said as she moved to rub her hand up his arm reassuringly. "I know you're not. Maybe that means... you don't want to be around. For the changes."

Cosmo's heart caught in his throat, and he could feel a tension between his shoulder blades, as if he was being torn in half. He slowly considered his next words. *I don't want to give you up*, he thought to say. *But I can't make myself just stand there while you wreck your life.*

"I don't want to give you up," he started. "But I-"

"Princess Saira," Kaiden broke in with a hushed voice, appearing out of nowhere and standing right beside them.

"Aah!" Saira gasped in surprise, and let go of Cosmo. "You sneak up everywhere!"

"Oh! I am sorry, but we must be without noise," Kaiden answered. "Move behind that rock there," he pointed. "You see four rocks I put in circle. As... seat." He swallowed. "And I have food. For after you have finished..."

"Yes, yes, I'll go," Saira said quickly, moving off in the direction he pointed. Only fifteen paces away she disappeared behind the far side of the boulder.

Kaiden turned to Cosmo and offered him a green stalk of foliage. It looked like a simple green stick. He looked up at Kaiden's face quizzically. Kaiden took another stalk and put the end of it in his mouth, grinding down teeth to crack the skin before making a subtle sucking for the juices that were emitted. "It is sweet."

Cosmo did the same, and tried to gradually increase pressure on the stick until he felt the skin crack. It was much more effort than he'd anticipated, but the reward was instant and delicious – a burst of succulent syrup into his mouth. "Wow!" he exclaimed as he licked his lips and stared at the green stalk.

"Yes, it is.. uh... tasting," Kaiden tested the word. "I... think it...", he glanced at Cosmo for a word suggestion.

Cosmo looked at him with a wry smile. "Yummy."

Kaiden looked at him quizzically, not understanding the word.

"It tastes good," Cosmo explained. "Not what I expected biting into a stick. Do your rocks taste good too?"

The aboriginal male laughed out loud, forgetting himself for a moment before he covered his mouth with a hand to stifle the noise.

"What was that? A laugh?" Saira asked as she returned from behind the rocks. "Cosmo actually said something to make you laugh?"

"Yummy!" Kaiden said, trying out the word as he extended a green stalk to Saira.

Saira smiled and chuckled, taking the stick and staring at it for a moment.

"Here, like this," Cosmo said as he put the end of the stick in his mouth and bit down on it again, gradually increasing the pressure to crack its sheath. The juicy flavor exploded into his mouth again and he made a slurping sound as he tried to ensure none of it drooled onto his chin.

Saira mimicked the action and herself made a surprised face at the results. "Wow," she echoed Cosmo's initial assessment. "This... can you eat all of it? I mean, the whole stick?"

"Yes, it is good. We can eat it," Kaiden said, pausing to find the correct words again. "It will give... strength. Uh.. make aware..."

"Breakfast," Cosmo agreed. "Our morning meal."

"I think I'm going to like your village, Kaiden!" Saira exclaimed.

"Water?" Cosmo asked. "Did you find any while you were..."

"Can you hear?" Kaiden returned with a query.

They were silent and listened for a moment.

"No," Saira said. "I can't hear anything except maybe the breeze of the wind."

Kaiden frowned. "I am sorry, Princess Saira. It is like your eyes and the seeing in dark." He looked as if he felt sorry for them that their senses were so dulled. "There is water nearby. Come from lake. The rains – they make more water than lake can hold."

"A waterfall?" Cosmo asked. "That's perfect. We can get a drink there."

"Yes, it is good." Kaiden pointed in the direction back towards the lake. "It is not far, from my hearings."

They walked in the direction Kaiden indicated through brush and gathering trees and foliage until finally Saira and Cosmo could both hear the sound from the water running over rocks.

The lake they had fallen into the previous evening was ringed by rock, but drained its overflow into a set of two waterfalls. The first was high and separated by a deep pool from the second much shorter one, which bottomed into another shallower pool. Below the second pool the waterway evened out into a narrow rocky riverbed.

As the trio approached the top of the first waterfall through some leafy trees, Kaiden grabbed their arms and stopped their progress. "Slow. We must walk slow. If Gorig are drink we must move on. Far away to another place."

Saira nodded, and reached out to grab Kaiden's hand. Cosmo sighed.

"Couldn't we smell them if they were here?" Cosmo asked.

"No. Wind is wrong here. It is danger. They can smell us, but we cannot smell them. But to go around, it is long walk."

Kaiden and Saira moved forwards, gradually through the trees to the perimeter of the clearing around the waterfall. Both Saira and Cosmo could see his ears move and his nose work the air as he scanned for movement with wide eyes. "We can move to top," he said cautiously after a moment. "Drink at top and see below."

Still holding Saira's hand Kaiden moved them forwards into the clearing around the top of the waterfall. Cosmo trailed warily, watching his footing on the flat rocks and occasionally looking back at the shelter of the trees. The roar of the rushing water masked out any subtle sounds that might have been heard as they came to the edge.

Cosmo was ten feet behind them when they kneeled down together where the water went over. Kaiden watched Saira as she used a cupped hand to drink. A stream dribbled out of her hand and she laughed at herself. Cosmo had to smile.

All three of them heard the beep from the gun's power switch.

Kaiden grabbed Saira and yanked her close to him, and they both jerked their necks to look in the direction of the noise. Ogren stood twenty feet away along the rim of the falls. His smell protected by the wind, up until that moment any sounds he had made had been muted by the rumble of the rushing water. The dirty Human looked ragged, but was smiling under the flop of hair that came down from half his scalp. "Perfect!" He said out loud. "Two for one."

Cosmo didn't remember a single step of running the ten feet. He hit the bulk of the combined mass of Kaiden and Saira with all his own weight, hammering into them both in a desperate running dive and knocking them from their place.

The spike fired from Ogren's gun slammed into the rock exactly where they had been squatting, exploding into a starburst of glowing white metal shards that impaled themselves into Cosmo, Kaiden, and Saira. In a bundled mass, yelling and screaming in pain and surprise the trio flew over the precipice and tumbled through the air down the long fall into the deep pool below.

twenty

The Daedalus coasted low over the trees, heading north towards the Teeth of the Forest. It had taken Jalendra and Kem all their wits to be able to communicate with the ship captain – they still were not sure what precisely had happened.

Jalendra could read Kem's frustration from twenty feet away as he peered over the side of the ship into the black and gray expanse of the forest below them. She approached him and he turned quickly to look and shout past her at the captain the word he'd asked Jalendra for: "Low!" He stabbed downwards with a pointed finger.

"Aye, Low," the captain called back, clearly irritated at the twelfth time Kem had yelled the same thing at him. "Get any lower and ye'll have trees up yer nose ye daft bugger!"

Kem turned back with a growl, completely ignoring Jalendra.

"Master, if they fell–" she started in their own language.

"I am no longer your Master," he said bluntly.

Her breath caught and her heart seemed to stop in her chest for a moment. "Kem, I have found my power – the fire of my destiny, so you said." She had never pleaded with him but she knew she was doing so now. "It is more than we expected. Different. But I still need your teaching, to use it properly. Maresh can help, but she... she knows less about any fire... inside... than you do."

Kem was quiet for a moment, but when he spoke his voice was different and detached. "It is my failure. A failure I cannot imagine I have made – but I cannot understand any differently."

Jalendra was still confused by the radical emotions coming from a Felid she had only ever known to be reserved and hard. "Master, you have not failed me, or anyone in the village."

"I was wrong about you," he said, finally turning to face her. "I saw the fire in you and took it and molded it, whittled it as I would a piece of ironwood. The way that I thought – that I knew - was right."

His eyes were wet. When he spoke his voice sounded different – as if his throat was constricted. "The same way I knew what was right for Kaiden."

Jalendra stayed quiet. Watching him it was if she could see the cracks appear in his hard shell.

"His mother took him from me."

Jalendra's heart caught in her throat again, and she felt a sinking in her stomach. All she knew was that Kaiden's mother had died and his training had stopped. Kaiden never spoke of it and certainly Kem never did. Jalendra was perplexed and a burst of questions filled her mind, but she knew she needed to help Kem. She knew she would likely never get another chance to understand. "What happened?"

"He could not kill. Would not kill," Kem said in a creaking voice. "I forced him. He still would not. His mother– she... he told her he could not kill. She listened to him. I was angry. She took him away – away from the village. In the night they ran from me... and then... the Gorig found them."

Jalendra was speechless. She wanted to offer some kind of reassurance that letting out his pain was all right with her. That she would listen and not question him or judge whatever had happened. She almost never touched him except when they sparred – but now she daringly reached out to touch his shoulder, scared to death that he would shrug off her hand or smack it away. She persevered and her hand touched down on the thin cloth of his red robe. She could feel the vibration in his taut muscles. He tilted his head sadly downwards.

"I failed them. Kaiden's mother died protecting him from them, and protecting his destiny from me. And now I have failed you by distorting yours – taking you away from your true path."

Jalendra thought for a moment, but kept her hand resting on his shoulder. "But my path is not known. Even

Maresh agrees. Perhaps my power is best molded by you, even if it is weaker as a killing-"

"Your power is stronger!" he blurted, looking up to stare into her face. "Stronger by far. Jalendra - killing is simple. Easy. Anyone can do it, even with the weakest spirit and with no flame burning in their heart."

He was talking to himself as much as he was talking to her. Convincing himself of logic he seemed to have worked out a long time ago, and had hidden from himself.

"I cannot even imagine what your heart can do. I don't understand it, and could never master it – teach it. It is not in my nature or my destiny."

She looked at him, then down at her hand resting on his arm. She took a deep breath. "Look into my eyes," she said.

He blinked, and looked at her quizzically.

"Just look into my eyes and stay still. Trust me. I will not hurt you. I want... to show you. To help you understand."

Kem looked irritated – and then worried.

She closed her eyes, and reached down inside.

The yellow flames were there, ready for her if she wanted to grasp them. She was almost surprised at how easy it was to find them, to know they were there at her disposal. She felt their warmth and color, and a quick shudder at their purpose and meaning. She reached past, careful in her mind not to brush against them.

The red glow beneath was also familiar, but rushed up quickly to meet her. She held back, and as she would feel the heat of a fire with the palm of her hand, she tentatively brushed her mind against the tendrils of the flames there. The natural connection with her body followed, and she routed the feeling up through her heart, her arm, her hand touching Kem's shoulder.

She flicked opened her eyes and found him staring back at her. She focused and looked at him. Into him. She saw pain – deep, old pain that branched out and sank its teeth into every part of him. She guided her fire to it and nudged against it gently, the barest wisp of a touch.

His mouth fell open.

Jalendra heard his shuddered breath and saw his eyes widen, shocked and worried - frightened at what he felt.

She pulled back and gently let go of his shoulder, and calmly closed off the channels inside her, damping down the flames and releasing the desire to connect with her hearth. She relaxed and softly smiled at Kem.

The older Felid closed his eyes and his mouth, and pulled his arms up across his chest as he tilted his chin down. He took in a long, slow breath that Jalendra could hear.

"I have never...", he started. Then he swallowed hard. "I don't understand. You did something..."

"It is the same for me," she said softly. "If you are a failure... for not seeing this, then I am a failure for not feeling it. I need to find what is right for me. Do you think that makes me a failure?"

"No." Kem's response was emphatic. "No. You are not a failure."

"Neither is Kaiden," she added.

His chin came up and he stared at her, then subtly his clenched arms relaxed and he rubbed his shoulder where she had touched him. He nodded.

"I have to find him, Jalendra," he said in a detached voice. "I have to tell him that. I see it now."

The ship passed over thinning trees below them to the crags of sharp gray rocks, rapidly approaching the Teeth of the Forest. Jalendra and Kem both quietly turned and looked over the side to study the ground.

"Hey! Hey there! Look there!" Jalendra exclaimed.

twenty one

Cosmo's head burst through the surface of the water. The right side of his face felt like it was on fire - he cried out as searing pain ran down his sensitive ear and pulsed in his cheek. Instinctively, he tried to feel with his hand at the area and realized that something was stuck to him. But his head went under the water again, and he had to work for a frantic moment to keep himself from drowning. Luckily, he had fallen into the pool not far from its edge, and only needed a desperate stroke or two in order to put his feet onto a rocky outcrop under the water.

He reached up to his cheek again and pulled something away from his face – something that seemed to burn his fingers as he grabbed and looked at it. It looked like metal. *A spike shard*, he thought, wincing as he dropped it. He felt dizzy and weak, ready to pass out from nausea. He could feel blood flowing over his cheek where he had yanked out the metal.

"SAIRA!", he yelled, looking around desperately, then back up from where they had fallen. He expected to see the Human again, looking down on him as he had back on the boat – but without his glasses he didn't see anything but a blur. He couldn't make out anything except the line of the water and the roar of its progress as it came down to splash in the pool near him. He swung around in a full circle as he got out of the pool, eyes blearily scanning for the princess. Save for the water the air was still.

"SAIRA! KAIDEN!" He bellowed again, almost in a cry. *Where are they?! Have they been hit?!* He staggered out onto the rocks at the edge of the pool and continued to look around, trembling from shock. His face felt like it was melting, and the pain in his ear was so bad he continued to feel dizzy and nauseous.

Suddenly off to his left he saw movement, and turned his head. But the movement was in the sky – squinting he could see a dark shape hanging against the gray of the clouds. *A ship?* Water drained from his left ear and he heard the hum of power sails.

His heart leapt. "Hey!" he yelled, at first tentatively and then with all the air he could muster in his lungs. "HELP! HEY!" He waved his arms frantically, and ran over the rocks towards the dark shape in the sky. He squinted and blinked, trying to see if it changed, if it rotated or if the sound of the sails became different. Stepping on top of a large round rock next to him he waved and yelled a long, hooting cry off into the distance. "HEEEYYYYYYYOOOAAA!!!!!"

He swore he saw the shape change – at least on one edge. He cursed his addled eyes and rubbed them, then waved frantically with his arms, yelling one more time. It seemed to change again, and get thinner. *I did it!*

His mouth gaped, and he frantically looked around the edge of the pool, trying to find the princess and Kaiden again with his eyes. "They saw me! They're coming!" He jumped down from the rock onto the ground.

Four Gorig stood in front of him in a semicircle, huffing small clouds of heated breath from their nostrils. Cosmo's heart instantly turned to stone in his chest, his mouth dropped open and his eyes bulged. Each of the huge beasts seemed at least three times as big as he was, their arms were huge and their crunched–up gnarled faces seemed to brim with sharp white teeth.

They stared at him for a moment as if mystified by his behavior. Their prey ran – it always ran. Cosmo stood like a stone, blinked and looked at the four of them less than ten feet away, arms coming up to hold his hands protectively in front of himself in a useless gesture. The two black monsters in the middle growled in deep rolling clucking chuckles.

"Cosmo!" came Saira's yell.

His head jerked to look past the Gorig at the line of trees next to the pool. Saira and Kaiden stood there disheveled and sopping wet, with Kaiden's face and chest covered in blood. "Saira — ah, ha haaah. Aiii– I'm in troub–"

"*Karratu! Gorig Karratu!*" Kaiden yelled in the aboriginal language to get their attention. He moved in front of Saira and Cosmo could see burnt holes in his robe. He was gritting his teeth in pain but turned his head and said something quickly to Saira, who immediately looked distressed and angry at his suggestion. He spit blood and roared at her. "You run! Run now or die!"

She took a jerking step backwards, face contorted in fear as she obeyed. Then Cosmo lost sight of her behind the center two Gorig, who took slow steps towards him and grunted out heated growls. It was all he could do to step backwards, his hands still in front of himself protectively as his heels bumped against rocks and he lost his balance, falling sideways to the ground. He didn't even look – he scrabbled away at the ground and started to run. He ran like he'd never run in his life.

He heard a squealing behind him, and the heavy thumping of footfalls on the gravel and rock. Vibrations echoed through the air and he had to yell out – absolutely terrified that his life was ending. He turned left abruptly, feeling like he was in a psychotic version of a child's courtyard chase. A Gorig surged past him and slid across a flat rock, its talons scraping against its surface as it fought to change direction to follow him. The other Gorig was quicker, its claws finding Cosmo's back and raking down it – perforating what was left of his robe and tearing it away from his flesh. He screamed in pain but cocked his shoulders back, letting the rags of what was left of his soaking wet attendant's garb slip from his body. In his loincloth he fell and rolled, feet slipping and toes fighting to grab against the biting rocks for purchase. Barely catching the ground he surged upwards and put everything his wracked muscles had left into a dash. Only three steps and he was knocked off his feet to the right by a heavy figure. He knew it was over as he was hit – his breath catching in him as he waited for the tearing teeth against his throat.

Kaiden had him.

Two steps with Cosmo under an arm and he jumped – high in an arc through the air and over an open chasm. Cosmo's weight threw off Kaiden's balance and they fell sideways, rockcting down faster and faster thirty feet to slam into the water of the river. Cosmo completely lost any coherence of what was happening, and simply tried to find out which way was up. Both his arms struck out madly against the water and he felt one of them break free of the surface. Turning he kicked and his feet found the riverbed, allowing him to thrust his head and neck up into the air.

He immediately saw the black hulk of a Gorig with its claws buried into Kaiden's side and back, white teeth madly gnashing away to try to get at the Felid's throat. Kaiden tried to fight it off – shoving at it as he screamed out terrifying deep guttural sounds of anger and pain.

Another Gorig slammed into the river beside Cosmo and reared back its claws. He held up his arms and closed his eyes, wincing his face against the animal fury coming down on him.

There was a thudding of force through the air and a livid, shrieking scream of fury in front of him and he fell backwards, submerged in the river again for a moment. Breaking his face free of the water he gasped for breath and saw a dark brown and gray Felid in a flashing red robe hammering away at his attacker with pummeling, thumping fists. The scream came again but from beyond him, as a gray and black female Felid's primary talons slashed back and forth, spraying blood and flesh from the Gorig attacking Kaiden.

The Felid in red was thrown off the Gorig that had come for Cosmo, but he seemed to not even fall to the ground. Instead he bounced off the riverside and flew through the air to slam a kick into a third Gorig that had followed the first two. The fourth Gorig yelled out a battle cry as it emerged above him and leapt from the small cliff Cosmo and Kaiden had fallen from.

Nothing in his life could ever have prepared Cosmo for the carnage he witnessed in and around the river. Kaiden's blood spurted from his wounds into the water and he tried to back away, but the Gorig on top of him ferociously continued its advance. The female warrior slashed with her hands and kicked with her feet, screaming as she finished off her first adversary and turned to inflict devastating blows onto the next one. And the huge male in red bounced and flitted from one target to the next – taking a cut from a claw or the swat of a heavy arm but never seeming to feel any of it, and never stopping his attack for one instant.

Cosmo kicked his feet and jumped towards the river's edge – trying to get out of the way and remove himself as a target. He was barely able to pull himself to shore when the huge heavy body of a Gorig slammed into the rocks next to him, its eyes wide in death as its head lolled on a broken neck.

"Kaiden!" he heard the female Felid yell. "*Kaiden los vardari! Vardari!*" Cosmo rolled and came up to his weak shaking knees, looking over the stinking body of the Gorig with a gaping mouth and wide eyes. The male Felid in red was on top of a third Gorig, his hand on its throat as his face was twisted into a deep grimace. The female had slashed her first Gorig to death and had broken the neck of the one next to Cosmo. He saw her turn to rush to Kaiden's side as he floated face down in the river. The fourth Gorig was crying yelps of pain, loping away down the river as it retreated.

"*Kaiden! Mai Varadi! Kaiden!*" the woman cried loudly, her distraught face breaking into a horrified mask as she pulled Kaiden up and clutched at his bloodied cheeks.

Saira, Cosmo thought blearily as he sat, slumped in total exhaustion. *Where is Saira?*

twenty two

Jalendra's mind screamed at the sight of Kaiden. She turned him face up and wrapped an arm around his neck to assess the worst injuries. Blood came from his head, his chest, his arms. His robe was burnt with flecks of metal and his right ear had a fresh hole burnt right through it. His head lolled and his pupils were dilated and no breath came from his mouth or nose. A steady stream of crimson colored water washed away from his mouth and nose.

Kem grabbed at his son, his own blood dripping from a deep cut on his face as he heaved for breath after the exertion of the fight. "He does not breathe!" Kem yelled. "Kaiden!" He pulled Kaiden close, and put his face down next to his son as the younger Felid floated in the shallows. Jalendra grabbed the back of Kaiden's neck to help, and tilted back his head. Holding Kaiden's body with one hand Kem pinched his son's nose shut and placed his lips gingerly over the younger

Felid's. He blew hard once and withdrew and listened for an outrush of air.

A gurgling came from the young Felid.

Kem urgently repeated the action, blowing air into Kaiden's lungs to replace the water. A strong gurgle and his son's legs spasmed. Water red with blood bubbled from his mouth then blew out in a spray with the air Kem had forced into him. The younger Felid's eyes closed hard in a wince, but he did not breathe in on his own.

"Kaiden! Kaiden, come on!" Jalendra yelled.

Once more Kem surged forward and blew air into his mouth, then withdrew and slapped Kaiden's cheek.

Kaiden blew out more reddened water then finally sucked in breath on his own with a desperate "hrrrreeeeeeek!" He gurgled and spat, the muscles of his neck clenching and releasing in quick succession over Jalendra's supportive hand. His chest went taut and he kicked out with his legs, but then his whole body went limp again.

"This is not working!" Kem shouted, terrified. "His lungs are damaged!" His voice cracked in desperation.

"Oh Kaiden!" Jalendra cried out. She pulled him away from his father by the neck and wrapped her other arm around him, bringing her face down against his cold cheek. Then she shut her eyes, trying to force out the world and reach inside.

But the world clawed at her. It stung and it crushed down in its fury. Her injuries from fighting the Gorig loudly demanded her attention, her lungs burned from the exertion of the fight, and her legs and feet shuddered from the cold of the water of the stream she stood in.

She shoved it all away and drove her mind down into the blackness of her spirit. The yellow flames raced up at her, billowing out and threatening to consume her, racing to connect with the death that they felt approaching through her arm. Kaiden's death.

She split the flames, not avoiding them but diving through them without reservation, without thought of their corruption and burning purpose. She knew what was underneath.

The red flame was hers.

She yanked it upwards, mastering it as a wild animal and yet partnering with it – embracing the truth and the purpose of her destiny. The yellow flames of wanton death were blown backwards by the overwhelming power as the red surged up. Without a thought she channeled it, routed it, and delivered it into and through her hand, feeling it flow into Kaiden's body.

Her eyes flew open and all she could see were Kaiden's eyes - the black pools ringed with amber. All she could think about was his life, about all she had to tell him, about all she wanted to share with him. How she never would ever let him go again.

Kaiden's mouth came open and he suddenly vomited reddened water. He winced his eyes shut and then coughed, pulling in breath and then coughing again. With one hand he grabbed his father's robe, while the other flailed out to instinctively try to steady himself as he floated in the water. His legs came under him and he staggered.

Kem grabbed him and pulled him up. Enveloping him with his strong and wide arms, he pulled his son close and held him tightly. The older Felid's face contorted and his chest shook as he cried.

twenty three

How can this get any worse? Ogren's mind screamed at him. *How did I let that happen?* It should have been the simplest of shots, easily taking out both the princess and the aboriginal. All he would have had to do after that is kill the attendant. *I am the most useless dung-faced fop at this hands-on stuff.*

Right after realizing he'd failed with his shot, he scrambled down the hill next to the waterfall, half falling on some of the more treacherous vertical sections. *Get down there,* he thought. *Get down there before they can regroup.* He knew he'd hit them – not directly, but with some of the shards. They'd be injured. Maybe he'd killed one of them, if they'd been hit right.

He heard the attendant Felid yelling names as he neared the bottom, and rushed through the foliage to try to get to him first and break his neck - or bash his head in with a rock. As he clambered through the thick brush he suddenly became aware of the hum of a ship's power sails. With the sudden gush of relief at possible rescue came a scream of urgency. *No good to go back if I'm gonna die when I get there!*

Just as he reached the thicket of trees at the edge of the clearing around the bottom of the first waterfall, he heard the aboriginal yelling. At least one of the words was 'run'. Ogren grimaced – *dammit! They're going to get away!*

As he surged through the last line of trees, Ogren was shocked to be almost run over by the fleeing princess. She skidded to a stop in front of him and gaped, dripping wet with wide eyes and a blanched face.

"Hello, your highness," Ogren said with a wicked grin as he stepped forward and grabbed the front of her tunic. His fist snapped forward and smacked a solid blow straight into her nose. She squeaked a cry and her head rocked backwards as she brought up her hands to defend herself. Blood spattered his hand but he held onto her tunic and pulled her forwards, jamming another blow into her gut below her protesting arms. The wind was knocked from her and she doubled over, unable to speak or scream. He let her hit the ground with a thud.

I think strangle, Ogren thought happily as he bent over her. He pulled her head back by the hair and looked into her gaping eyes as her body fought for breath that would not come. *Yep, strangle.*

His hands came comfortably around her throat – slowly and surely. His mind flashed back to the Felid in the dark room with the long knife, who took care and slow precision in his careful ministrations to kill. Through labored breathing he chuckled as he tightened his grip on her windpipe, understanding the thrill his employer had certainly experienced. Then he started to squeeze.

She convulsed and twisted as he cut off what little air she was getting, then reared up her waist and kicked out with her foot – right up between his legs. Everything in the world dropped from consideration as the pain rocked up from his groin through to an intense ball of agony in his bowels. He yelped and fell off her, rolling sideways and seething breath.

She was up – up and taking a step away from him before he could recover. He put down a knee and pushed himself up, but the wracking pain from his crotch caused his leg muscles to shudder and fail, and he toppled against the trees at the entrance to the clearing. He reached out desperately with his arm but only caught the slippery edge of her cape as she pulled her nimble thinner body another step away from him. *Dammit!*

He shoved his way through the pain, lumbering up and bouncing off a tree as he angrily growled and came after her. She screamed once out in the open. They would hear her. He tried to imagine for a moment that they would not, but he knew it was folly.

I screwed this up. Yet again.

Finally able to stand without wobbling, he fought through the pain and ran after her, locking eyes on her back as she tried desperately to get away. She screamed again and he had to look around as he ran after her – catching sight of the sky boat floating off to his right. *Game is up,* his mind pulsed. *They know I'm here.* His groin ached with pain as he ran after the princess, but he quickly caught up with her. His anger overrode any sense he had left – all he wanted to do was kill her. Smash her head against the rocks. *I'll work it out,* he thought quickly. *I don't care that they saw me. All I need to do is kill her. I'll get back north somehow. I'll walk if I have to.*

She abruptly stopped in front of him, turning to hold up her arms in a desperate but useless plea for him to stop. He was confused, but then saw that she stood at the precipice of a cliff face, at least a thirty foot drop onto rocks next to the river.

"Nobody can save you now," he growled in a low voice at her, hand coming to his groin to try to soothe the intense pain there. "You're dying – right now!"

"No!" Saira screamed as he came at her, trying to dart to her right so that she could run. He caught her easily – one hand on her arm and the other coming up to tightly and painfully grip her hair. Then he grunted and threw her like a rag doll over the side of the cliff.

She fell the thirty feet, screaming the whole way, until her body struck the rocks next to the river.

twenty four

Cosmo had heard Saira's cry, his eyes yanked away from the two aboriginal warriors clutching Kaiden. He looked up and saw her falling, tumbling over and over down onto the packed round stones near the river. And he heard the sickening crack as she slammed into the ground.

"Saira!" he screeched. "Aaa! Saira!" He jumped up, water splashing as he erratically surged through the river, desperate to reach her. Thoughts of Kaiden abruptly left him and for a moment all he could feel was the clenching of his stomach and thick nausea. Pictures of her body flashed through his mind – harrowing contortions and combinations of every way she had ever injured herself, in twelve cycles of attending to her.

He saw her and his knees collapsed, his hands shooting up to cover his gaping mouth.

She lay with her back cracked over a rock, leg twisted sideways at a sickening angle, and one arm brutally wrapped underneath her back. Her mouth was agape and her neck was twisted as she stared wild–eyed straight at him. But he could see her chest move as she fought blindly for breath, her concussed brain unable in any way to cope with the trauma of her body. *She's alive!*

But she was suffering. Far beyond any of his cuts and bruises, and anything he could imagine he had ever been through. He could see she was dying quickly – there was no way anyone could survive that trauma. He pressed his hands against his mouth to cover it in horror, and emitted a low haunting moan.

He had to look upwards from where she fell, eyes alighting instantly on a white blur. All he could make out in a split second was a half-head of hair. His addled eyes could not make out the face, but the familiarity of the head made it connect with the face from when he'd fallen from the boat. He would never forget that face in his life. The white blur dropped back from the edge and was gone.

Cosmo reached out tentatively to touch Saira, but couldn't for the life of him know how he could possibly do anything to help. Even moving her head could cause her more pain than she was already experiencing. He started to cry, tears rolling down his face in sobs he could not control. Blood from where the spike shard had impaled his cheek ran down and dripped off his chin, but all he could do was croak her name again and again and again. "Saira... Saira... Saira."

She choked once and her eyes seemed to find him for a moment, before defocusing again as blood started to drip from her ears and mouth. The rest of her body did not move at all, seemingly paralyzed.

"Help," Cosmo croaked, low and plaintive, barely a whisper as he looked furtively around in desperation. "Help!" There was nothing he could do – all he knew was silence and the layers of memory washing over him. How could it be over now? Like this?

"*Va verdik*," the female Felid spoke from behind him, through her own weakened and shaking voice. "She die now." She looked at Cosmo sadly.

He raised his arm and pointed at Saira, and the only words he could think of came to his lips. "Saira. She's... she's my..." He came forward, reaching to touch her hand as it lay flaccid against her side. Her breathing started to falter, and her eyes started to become wider. "My... child..." he sputtered.

"*Teona*," the female said softly.

twenty five

As Kaiden had stood and been taken into an embrace by Kem, Jalendra had sunk down on her side in the water, barely with enough energy to keep herself afloat. Her head swam and it had been hard to breathe. Her body seemed to want to give up – to pass out and fall away from the life force it had given. She had heard Kaiden coughing, trying to breathe on his own and recover. She'd relaxed - he was going to be all right.

Then the young warrior had heard Saira's cry and the horrible sound as the princess' body had struck the riverbed. The pitiful cries from the thin black northern Felid were overwhelming as he went straight to her.

Jalendra wanted to stand. She wanted to run towards the princess. To see how bad it was. She could feel the flickers of need in her heart to help. But she could hardly move, she could hardly think. She could barely breathe.

I have to try, she thought. Closing her eyes she drove herself to move, to stand. Dizzy, she almost fell over onto her face.

The fire that is given to stoke life is difficult to replace.

She heard Maresh's words in her head.

...the injury was too great... their power was not enough, and they were destroyed.

I can't, she said, even as she drew towards the black Felid and the crumpled form of the princess. *I can't. I don't have anything left.*

"Help!" the black Felid called out.

Jalendra looked down as she stumbled close to the pair, taken aback at the sight of Saira's body. There was no way. No way she could fix this. She would have to give more than she had given to Kaiden. And it would consume her. The flame of her destiny would burn her mind past repair. She knew at that moment something Maresh could not have known - the ancestors who tried to heal the planet must have realized they would fail. As Jalendra knew she would fail now, if she tried.

"*Va verdik*," she said, voice warbling in the aboriginal tongue. He looked up at her and she sadly looked down said the words in his language so he would understand. "She die now."

The ragged black northern Felid pointed at Saira, delirious with grief. "Saira," Jalendra heard. "My... Child."

She pushed away the thought of healing Saira. Shut it away from possibility as the word took her into herself, into her own needs. Her head turned and she looked back at the father and son.

Kem was still holding on tightly – even though Kaiden was healed Kem could not let go of his son. But just as Jalendra looked at them, Kaiden's head came away from Kem's shoulder and he looked blearily at her.

She saw her children. Their children.

"*Teona*," Jalendra said the word in the aboriginal tongue, almost a whisper. She turned and looked down on Cosmo and Saira, and the welling in her heart drove her towards her destiny.

twenty six

Cosmo was jarred by the aboriginal female's sudden movement to kneel next to him. She held out her hand and tucked it around the back of Saira's neck, moving the princess' head. He started to mutter a protest, but instinctively knew the southern Felid was trying to help. If it was to make Saira's pain stop, he would let her. His heart twisted in his chest as he saw the aboriginal look into Saira's eyes in concentration. Saira had been his charge, his life for so long. He could not fathom a world without her.

He saw Jalendra lean in above the princess to strongly and firmly wrap her other arm around Saira's broken back. She lifted the northern Felid into her arms and held her close and tightly. Then the aboriginal closed her eyes. Cosmo watched for a moment as there was no sound. No movement, not even the rustle of wind or the bubble of the river.

Saira croaked out a deathly rattle of words "Ja... len...“

Jalendra pulled back her head, and nose to nose flicked open her eyes to stare into those of the princess.

Saira's legs shook and her breath suddenly came rushing into her lungs with a painfully high pitched squeal. Then she went rigid as her eyes blinked widely, looking up into the other female's face with a look of shocked wonder. Cosmo's mouth dropped open as Saira's arms shot out to the sides and then came up – no longer broken or twisted, as she gripped Jalendra's scratched and bloodied shoulders. Then the warrior cried out as well, a hurtful moan as her eyes winced shut and her arms and body suddenly went limp. She abruptly let go of the princess and fell away, collapsing into a heap on the ground.

Saira's bottom touched the rocks below her and she heaved for breath, looking about madly as she was stunned to find herself sitting of her own accord. No more blood came from her mouth or ears, and she blinked her huge eyes and swallowed, running her hands over her body as if she was checking for injuries that were no longer there.

Cosmo was speechless, but could not contain a rush of absolute relief as he grabbed Saira with his arms and pulled her to him. "What?! What happened?! Saira – you. You're all – all right?"

"I– I was dying. I barely knew it." The princess' breath came in starts and she was shaking. "What I had left was fading away so fast. It hurt – it hurt so much, Cosmo. But I see it now... I can see how I... I was lying there. She brought me back. Took it away – all the pain. It's gone."

"I thought you were gone," he said as he shuddered through tears. "Daughter of my heart I thought you were gone."

"Oh Cosmo!" Saira burst out and held him in a crushing embrace. She started to cry as the rush of words took her, shaking uncontrollably. "My sweet Cosmo!"

"It's all right," he soothed. "It's all right. Shh... I'm right here. I won't leave. I-"

"JALENDRA!" Cosmo heard a deep yell. He jerked his head around to see Kaiden and the red-robed older Felid splashing in a run through the stream and onto the shore towards them.

"JALENDRA! *KA DEMI*!" Kaiden pleaded. He reached the female first, rolling her limp body over on the rocks.

"What did she do?!" Cosmo called out, incredulous. "What – how did she do... what she did?"

Saira grabbed Cosmo's hand and held it, her voice a worried garble as she watched. "Did – Cosmo is she...?"

Kaiden sat next to Jalendra and pulled her up, wrapping his arms around her and pulling her face next to his. Her body was absolutely limp. He rocked for a moment, then was still. He whispered words Cosmo could not understand into her ear.

"*Der Kemmick*", the older Felid said breathlessly. "*Der Kemmick, Kaiden. Vas ah tu, pret*".

Kaiden put one hand at the back of her head and gently withdrew to look at Jalendra's face, brushing his cheek along hers. When he spoke his voice was calm.

"*Vasha*. *Vasha Jalendra*." He smiled and gently placed his lips on hers, kissing her softly and slowly.

Cosmo saw Jalendra's chest suddenly rise, and her mouth move on its own as she kissed him back.

twenty seven

Ogren moved past the last crumbling hill, spots of foliage disappearing and bare rock turning from its gray to flat black. Everywhere he looked was dark char.

The Dead Zone. The Ash. Those and the other names for it rolled through his mind.

He had managed to find a small stream and fill his water flask, but it felt puny and useless on his waist. He had no cloak, no tools, no supplies of any kind. The empty spike gun was useless and he'd tossed it into the brush, but he'd foraged through the last mile of the Teeth of the Forest and found some green and black berries. Unfortunately, he had no idea if they were edible or poisonous.

Doesn't really matter, he admitted to himself. *When the time comes, it'll be eat them or die anyway.*

He trudged forwards reluctantly, looking around at the seared hills and mounds of blackened gravel.

She's dead, he reminded himself. *I've already won.* It would have to be enough to keep him going.

twenty eight

Cosmo began to gingerly place his spare set of glasses on his face, but winced at the pain as they touched his cheek. He gritted his teeth and steeled himself against the searing feeling, and hissed out his breath. Finally he was able to open his eyes, and was instantly grateful to finally be able to see again. He looked around at the compartment under the ship's forecastle and marveled at how much had happened since he had last been in the space. He then drew his spare robe from his case and began to put it on.

"We can't tell my father," Saira said as she stood just outside the entrance.

Despite the pain Cosmo chuckled. He was still elated by the princess' miraculous and apparently almost instantaneous recovery, but could not believe they would get away with omitting any part of the full description of their little adventure. "Yeah," he deadpanned. "Uh-huh. Sure."

"Cosmo we can't tell him or he'll never let me out of the palace again!"

"We have to. At least about the assassin. Describe that Human to him so that if-"

"He's stuck out there in the forest. He came on the ship with us. How is he going to get back? And those... Gorig things. They'll probably get him."

"You want to bet your life on that?"

She crossed her arms over her chest and tilted down her chin in defeat. "No."

"You should change your clothes. You bled all over them and you're about to meet the rest of Kaiden's village."

She looked down at herself, at the stains of blood on her outfit and the rips in the fabric where bones had traumatically broken out. She closed her eyes and shuddered.

"You're ok now. I don't know how, but you're ok."

"I am. It's like... it's like it never happened," Saira said, shaking her head in disbelief. "I wouldn't believe me if I told the story. But you..."

She gingerly held out her hand at Cosmo's face but did not touch it. He slit his eyes and grimaced. "I am ok for the moment – not like I have a choice. At least the captain said they have healers at the village." He sighed and looked past the princess across the deck. He swallowed hard and his voice dropped low. "But she's not ok."

Kaiden sat on the floor at the far end of the ship's main deck, with Jalendra seated comfortably across his lap. She leaned against his chest and had her eyes blearily half lidded in exhaustion, but was breathing steadily. Kem was next to them, kneeling on the hard deck boards with his face a mask of concern. Cosmo and Saira could see Kaiden talking softly to the female aboriginal, coaxing her to respond.

"No, she's not ok" Saira said in regret. "But she's better already than she was. She's moving her head, see? I think... I think she's just drained. More than we could ever imagine. From what she did." The princess contemplated them for a moment. "He loves her," she said softly. "*Vasha*".

Cosmo looked over at the princess, expecting sadness. But she was smiling.

"Yes," he said with a long pause. "Not sure you want to get in between those two."

"Those three," she agreed and extended his statement. "The older male is Kaiden's father."

"How do you know that?"

"I can tell. It's how they are. They're- the three of them- they're a family."

Cosmo moved to exit the hold, and stood up at the entrance to come out next to Saira. At the last moment he jerked to a stop as he felt the touch of the princess' hand on the crown of his head. He looked up through his brows and saw he'd almost smacked his head. Again.

"Taking care of me?" he said with a smile as he moved forward and out of the compartment.

"If you'll take care of me," she bartered.

"You sure you want me to?"

"Only if it's what you want. You're not my attendant anymore, but you can have any position you want in the palace."

"How about... House Master?" he asked with the lilt of an eyebrow. He gritted his teeth against a flash of pain from the protestation of the small muscles in his forehead.

"Oh! That's a great idea! Oh Cosmo, you'd be great at that! And you'd be close and I'd see you all the time. Master Darris is old, and he's been so tired lately. I'm sure he'll retire if I ask him."

"I don't know, sounds kind of unlikely. You might have to promise your father something in return to have him agree."

"I don't care! We have to do that! I'll demand my father does that."

He slowly smiled, and put an arm around her as they walked towards the Felids on the far side of the deck. She matched his stride and put her head on his shoulder.

"Then I know what I want," Cosmo said.

twenty nine

Thistle was on his knees in the dark room, his breathing coming in short gasps under the cloth bag over his head. There was no one else in the room. He knew why he was here. He knew what was going to happen. They had put him here and let him wait, to let the terror slowly destroy his mind.

The door opened and a shadow fell across the light, and then slowly the door closed again. Thistle's breath caught but he said nothing. He didn't try to bargain for his life – he didn't try to make an argument for why he had failed in his task. He was sure it didn't matter now. He was sure he was going to die.

The bag came off and he looked up, face covered in sweat, at the fiery green eyes of the Felid he had hoped he would never see so close again. Thistle's glance flicked instinctively to the bone handle of the knife – its smooth whiteness visible even in the dim of the room.

"Mister... Thistle..." the deep voice said with its hint of rasp. "So sorry to see you here today, with no sign of your friend Ogren. And the princess still very much alive, despite what we heard over the comm was a very big adventure."

When he spoke, Thistle's voice warbled a stutter he could not keep still. "C–can we g–get this ov–v–ver with p–please?"

The Felid shrugged and took out his knife, sliding it unceremoniously out of its sheath and rolling it in his hand once as he looked down with a stone face on the Kesten. He sighed and put the knife up to the male's chest, moving it only a tiny bit before resting it on the proper spot.

Thistle grunted at the touch, animal instinct shaking out a growl of what he thought would be his last words in defiance at the white–robed noble in front of him: "You will never be king."

The Felid stopped and stepped back to look quizzically at Thistle. He even pulled the knife away to let its weight hang easily from his wrist. The Kesten gulped for breath, surprised he was not already on the floor in a pool of his own blood.

"King?" his captor hung the question in the air. He smiled in jest. "Why would I want that? The king has to talk to people. He has to listen to the people. He has to deal with the people."

Thistle coughed, completely confused as he continued to shake in his terror.

"The people are stupid," the Felid said bluntly. He glanced up and sniffed the room, the aroma around them. "The people stink. I can't even stand the taste of the air in here. I... hate... the people. All of them."

The knife came up and he waved it once in front of the Kesten's face, before taking up his stance before the male and carefully placing the point of his knife at the precise location on Thistle's chest.

"Then what do you wanah–haAAA!" the Kesten yelled as the knife started to pierce his flesh. It twisted into a gargling yell as the Felid pushed harder and yet moved slower, the point of his blade doing its duty to cut past skin, bone and muscle into the heart. Thistle screamed and convulsed as his Felid murderer stood over him and twisted his knife to end the Kesten's life in agony.

The withdrawal of the blade's length was quick and silent – a slick sound denoted at the end by the splat of Thistle's limp body onto the floor. The Felid then wiped his knife and carefully placed it back in its sheath, gazing down pitifully on the dead Kesten.

"I want a broken king," he said aloud to the dead male. "One who has only my voice at his ear. So... I suppose it's 'try try again'."

He turned and coughed once, and once again. He stepped to the door and opened it, speaking in a croak to his attendants. "I am still ill. Bring me water."

"Yes, Lord Jasper."